MUTAGEN

A NOVEL BY MICHAEL COLE

SEVEREDPRESS

MUTAGEN

WWW.SEVEREDPRESS.COM

ISBN: 978-1-923663-01-5

CHAPTER 1

The predator had sunk its teeth into its helpless prey, sawing skin and muscle tissue.

Willy Phelps watched the line tighten. He leaned back in his fishing chair and pulled on his rod. The hook sank into the roof of the shark's mouth, securing the barb.

The fight had begun. Judging by the force of the pull, this shark was a healthy one. Good. The last two were thin, weak, and sickly. He still took the fins—his customers weren't necessarily the picky sort. But there was nothing to worry about regarding this bad boy. The fight was what Willy loved most. That, and the cash the fins brought him.

He looked around before turning on his deck light. The cops usually weren't out this late, and even if they caught him, they probably wouldn't care. But there was that stupid tree-hugging conservationist officer from Kansas. The bastard was already up in everybody's business, including Willy's. Up until last week, Willy used a drift net to catch sharks. Easy work. Simply line it with bait, leave it out for a day or two, then come back to it. Usually, the sharks that got themselves snagged were dead by the time he hauled them in. Easy work. Reel, slice, discard bodies. He loved the thrill of old-fashioned fishing, but the reality was it took time to get the necessary number of fins for his buyer. And Willy knew all the right spots to catch them by the dozens.

Then that piece of shit Julian Reed showed up in his coastal community, shoving his badge in everyone's face, talking about how overfishing is killing the population. Environmental Protection Agency. As far as Willy was concerned, the guy was nothing more than a glorified dog catcher.

That attitude didn't stop him from being cautious. In the dead of night, his boat light would stick out like a sore thumb. And he didn't put it past Reed to be out prowling in the dark in search of illegal trappers in the hope of catching them in the act.

It was only a matter of pure luck that Willy wasn't caught near that drift net. Two days ago, Reed had discovered it, along with the twenty dead blue shark and hammerheads that went after the bait. Willy was smart enough not to leave any labels or identifiers that would link him to it, though it was clear Reed suspected him. A few fishing buddies warned him to lay low for a while, but he couldn't resist the temptation of that almighty dollar. The buyers spoke louder than his friends, and they spoke with cash. So, it was time to work the old-fashioned way—at night, with a good ol' reel and line.

He switched on the light, illuminating the aft deck of the *Round Five*, named for the one shining moment in his short-lived boxing career.

The shark went with the line, allowing itself to be reeled in fifteen feet before diving. It couldn't outmuscle the string that prevented it from darting, so maybe there was refuge in the depths.

The rounded fisherman leaned forward, allowing the fish a few feet of line, waited a few moments for it to tire out, then pulled back on the rod. Lean forward, reel, tug, repeat.

"You're not getting away that easy."

The fish broke the water. Willy pointed his spotlight on it. A hammerhead. Ten feet long. Not a bad catch. Just twenty more feet of line to reel in, then he'd snare the bastard with his pole and hook, haul it aboard, slice its fins off, then toss the eel-like body into the water.

For a moment, it looked as though the shark had given up. Its grey skin resembled silver in the spotlight as it slowly glided along the surface. A predator of the sea, it was no match for the technology of man. It seemed to gaze at the thirty-five-foot fishing vessel with a hint of resignation. Or, maybe it was the booze that Willy drank. After three beers, his imagination tended to go wild. After five, he often thought he noticed human characteristics in fish. Frowns, smiles, and so forth. It made him the butt of a hundred jokes at the Seaweed Bar, where he and his buddies met up every other night. More than once, Willy considered the fact that if he didn't go there so often, he'd be thousands of dollars richer and thirty pounds lighter.

Gonna be richer once I have this fish aboard.

He reeled the shark another ten feet, then reached for the prod. The hammerhead was barely moving at this point. Should be easy work to get the hook on it.

In the blink of an eye, the fish exploded into action. The rod slipped from Willy's grasp and shot for the gunwale. The pudgy fisherman ran after it, tripping over his own gear in the process. He heard the *clang* of the reel hitting the gunwale, then a splash as it hit the water.

"Son of a bitch!"

He rose to his feet, only to hear another, larger splash. The sound was the first thing he noticed, then the rocking of the boat. The *Round Five* was not simply wobbling in slight waves—these were swells rivaling those generated by hurricane force winds.

Or those created by a massive object hitting the water.

Willy pointed his spotlight. He saw movement along the surface. The hammerhead was drifting with the swells, roughly thirty feet straight ahead. The body rolled, revealing the fleshy wound where its tail previously connected to its body behind the dorsal fin. He was looking at half a shark.

The remains were starting to sink. The only reason it was there to begin with was the fact that it had been *thrown* there.

Something emerged under it. Submarine-shaped—with fins. He saw the parting of jaws, then the breaking of water. Huge green eyes peered over the water before being obscured by nictitating membrane. Two-inch teeth pieced the remaining hammerhead. The shaking of the jaws shredded the fish to ribbons.

Willy stared in stunned silence as the new arrival consumed his prize. It was like nothing he had ever seen before. Skin covered in scythe-like denticles, eyes green as radioactive sludge, a caudal fin as tall as a man. This was no great white. Hell, it wasn't even the mythical megalodon. This was something else entirely.

For the first time in his life, Willy was driven by a force more powerful than cash.

Fear.

He started the engine and pointed the boat toward home.

CHAPTER 2

"Go kill yourself, you piece of shit."

When Agent Julian Reed first flashed his badge at the belligerent Mark Wall, the response was "I got one of those for my bachelor party. Except mine said boob inspector." When Julian inquired about the illegal drift nets and traps, Mark's replies escalated to "mind your business, cowboy," and "go back to Kansas and stuff yourself with some corn fritters."

It was when Julian boarded Mark's vessel, the *Lineman*, that things got really heated. By the time Mark realized the agent was approaching, he was already in the middle of bringing in his drift net. Entwined in the mesh fabric were over a hundred flounder and mackerel, most of which were dead or dying. In addition to those unlucky creatures were two Caribbean reef sharks, a bigeye thresher, a lemon shark, and a hammerhead. All of them dead, having entangled themselves in the mesh and suffocated.

Mark and his mate, Glenn—an ex-con with bad prison ink covering both arms—knew they were caught. Julian had seen them in the local bars of the Gulf Coast village of Pelican Grove. In public, they were crude, not necessarily disorderly, but sometimes teetered on the verge.

The fishermen of Pelican Grove had little patience for the agent. As far as they were concerned, he was a tree-hugging hippie who was out to wreck their livelihoods. The only people who didn't seem to mind his arrival were the hotel staff, and even they seemed wary of the thirty-seven-year-old agent.

Word of his arrival spread like a virus. Many people in the small town looked at him as though he was an alien infiltrator out to eliminate their way of life. His midwestern attire made him stand out like a sore thumb in their neighborhood. Down here, nobody wore denim shirts and cowboy boots. Nobody except outsiders, at least. And those who came to Pelican Grove stood out like a sore thumb, for the village did not get many visitors. It was a simple fishing village with little to offer tourists. They usually went to the Keys, Port Charlotte, or Fort Myers.

Julian would have rather gone to any one of those places. Being an agent for the Environmental Protection Agency, he went where the work was. In this case, it was Pelican Grove. It was not the worst place he had ever seen. It was leagues better than the cesspool that was San Francisco and various other densely populated crime-ridden areas in the nation. But it wasn't the best place either. Not even close.

Aside from the beach areas, it was a pretty stale location. When Julian first arrived, he thought he went back in time thirty years. Most of the boats were at least that old. Most of the land-based vehicles weren't much better. Even the police interceptors were covered in rust and had mufflers barely attached to their undersides. Then there was the architecture. Aside from a few construction sites, most of it was decades old.

His first night was spent staring at the water-stained ceiling tiles in his hotel room. Hopefully, the roof leak that caused them had been fixed. Hopefully he would not have to find out.

That was a concern for later. For now, he had a jackass poacher to deal with.

"Cry all you want, Mr. Wall," he said. "But facts are the facts. You're under arrest for the slaughter of protected species, and the illegal use of drift nets. Turn around and put your hands behind your back."

Mark squared up with the agent, using his superior height as a method of intimidation. It only partially worked. Julian was not one who relished altercations. He preferred the scientific aspects of his work, such as conducting water tests and rescuing animals from traps. Every so often, a perpetrator had to be arrested.

The agent went to take a step back, only to abort the retreat and hold his ground.

"I'm not going to tell you again, Mr. Wall." He kept the first mate in his peripheral while he spoke. Glenn was standing on the flying deck, with one hand on the ladder bar. Julian could envision the wheels turning in his head. Both fishermen clearly cared little for the rule of law or the potential consequences of their actions. Worse, they probably figured they could throw him overboard and get off scot free. Knowing the local sheriff, he would probably buy into any bullshit story they threw his way.

'Oh, the poor agent fell overboard. We tried to save him, but he hit his head on the hull and drowned.'

It made him wonder what other skeletons these men had in their closets.

"Watch yourself, Agent Boy," Mark said. "In case you haven't noticed, you're not in Kansas anymore. You're in *my* neighborhood. Out here, we don't take kindly to outsiders sticking their noses into our business. We scrap and claw to put food on our dinner plates. We don't come from places of privilege like you, pretty boy."

Julian wrinkled his nose and licked his lips. Now he was getting irritated, firstly at the false assumptions regarding his character and background, second at the nonstop attitude he had endured since his arrival. This fisherman—this poacher—had broken the law right in front of him and had the gall to act as though he was the victim.

"I suggest you watch yourself," Julian warned. "In case you've forgotten, I'm the man with the gun. So, go ahead. Threaten me again. See how that works out for you." He turned his eyes to Glenn. "And as for you, I suggest you keep that block of a jaw of yours shut, or I'll shut it for ya."

With his left hand, Julian removed an expandable baton from his belt. A press of a button revealed twenty inches of black steel designed specifically for causing pain.

Mark cracked a small grin. He didn't think the agent had it in him. The sudden inhale through his nostrils suggested he was considering taking the agent up on his challenge. Julian had one hand resting on his Glock, the other on an expandable baton strapped to his left hip. The fisherman's eyes shifted downward at the weapons, his mind choreographing every particular scenario.

Ultimately, he went with the path of least resistance.

Much to Julian's relief, Mark turned around and put his hands on the transom. The agent pulled those arms behind Mark's back and slapped some cuffs over his wrists. He helped the suspect cross over the portside gunwale to his cruiser.

"Take a seat," Julian said, pointing to a chair on the aft deck.

"Feeling like a big man now, Agent?" Mark replied. "Arresting innocent civilians who are struggling to make a living?"

Julian dug a coin out of his pocket and flipped it onto Mark's lap. "Here's a quarter. Call someone who cares." He turned to face Glenn, who remained on the flying deck of the *Lineman*. "I'll let you off the hook, being as you were working under Mr. Wall and I technically did not witness you handling the illegal net. That said, only as long as you take this boat to the police harbor. Keep these specimens on the deck. You get rid of them, you will officially be destroying evidence and will be charged with interfering with an investigation. Understand me?"

Glenn's dark, unblinking eyes bored holes into Julian's skull. For a moment, Julian wondered if he was going to have a problem with this man too. Glenn was smaller than Mark, but was clearly not a soft man. His hands alone looked as though they could crush metal. Glenn was not the type who spent half of his hours in front of a computer screen. He was a laboring individual who was likely no stranger to pain.

After a silent, tense moment, the first mate nodded.

Julian's sigh of relief was a little too audible, much to Mark's amusement.

"What's the matter, Agent? Afraid you were gonna have to call for backup?"

Julian's first instinct was to shoot him a glare. He resisted, knowing such a reaction was exactly what Mark was looking for. He untied the ropes which held the two vessels together, then ascended to the flying bridge of his vessel and started the engine, not offering any response to his cuffed suspect. He snatched the speaker mic from the console and pressed its transmitter.

"Boat October-515 calling the Traverse County Sheriff's Department. This is Agent Julian Reed, over."

In the moments that followed, he could envision the dispatcher rolling her eyes and griping about the 'pesky tree-hugging agent begging for assistance yet again'.

"Go ahead."

The tone confirmed his suspicions. Even the dispatchers were not fond of his presence. From what Julian could tell, the deputies in Pelican Grove were the epitome of the donut-eating cop stereotype. For the most part, they sat around, save for a few scattered patrols, and did next to nothing. Whenever their assistance was requested, they responded as though somebody asked them to donate a kidney.

Apparently, it was the best deal the town could get. It was so poor and run-down, they did not bother forming their own local police department. Traverse County was tiny to begin with, and most of the so-called action was in Pelican Grove.

"I've arrested one of your locals for poaching south of Cozy Rock. I'm gonna be bringing him in to the harbor. Have the sheriff meet me out there, will ya?"

There was another few moments of silence.

"Ten four."

Julian shook his head and placed the mic down. "Well, excuse me. Sorry I asked."

He started his engine and waited for Glenn to finish bringing up the *Lineman's* anchor. The ex-con moved across the boat in a robotic manner, displaying zero emotion or personality. Julian watched as he climbed to the flying bridge and started the boat's engines.

The *Lineman* roared to life, spewing black exhaust from its pipes. Its helmsman steered it east towards the harbor at ten knots.

Julian put pressure on the throttle and followed him. As he went, he kept his eyes on the boat and the water surrounding it. A flash of silver in the waves caught his eye. A dead fish was caught in the surf, its body discolored from lack of blood flow. He slowed down and gave a closer look at the dead animal as he passed by it. The gills were purple, the tailfin was small for its size, and the belly was bloated. The latter was common for dead aquatic life, for gases in the stomach usually expanded. The gills and fins, however, were indicative of dioxin poisoning.

It was something he had seen too much of during his investigation. Someone was dumping something in these waters and poisoning the sea life. Finding out who was doing it and where were the top of Julian's list of priorities. Hopefully before it got any worse.

Whoever was doing it picked this area deliberately. Knowing the people of Pelican Grove, they were more than willing to turn a blind eye to any wrongdoing. Especially if there was some coin being tossed their way.

CHAPTER 3

Julian Reed endured a long list of snide remarks from Mark Wall during the return trip. There were shots at his slight Kentuckian accent, his country attire, some remarks about being bred from cousins, and more. It became easy to tune out after the third or fourth quip. After that, it was nothing more than a background ambience.

After a few insults, Mark went with something new. "You carry that thing to feel tough? Or do you use it to pleasure a woman? I think it's safe to say it's the only functional stick in your possession."

Julian glanced downward. His hand was instinctively resting on the expandable baton strapped to his left hip. He always carried one ever since his rookie year as a small-town cop in Kansas. 'Small town' was a term generally used to refer to any non-urban area. In fact, many of those 'small towns' comprised of reasonably large populations spread over many miles. But in the case of Hesperia, Kansas, it was legitimately a small town. Tiny town would have even sufficed in describing it. It made for easy policing. Much of his shifts were hanging out at the local fish and tackle shops.

In those early years, he had the typical craving of adventure. He believed he was wasting his potential. Being a lover of the outdoors, he chose to pursue a criminal justice career in environmental services.

Julian learned very quickly that adventure was not what it was cracked up to be. He saw a lot of things he wished he hadn't; dead animals, land-based and marine, that were killed due to human negligence and exposure to pollution. He met a lot of people he wished he hadn't; people like Mark Wall, and others who abused dogs and tortured wildlife.

In his rookie year as an EPA agent, he accompanied his training officer to a hunting site. The suspect in question evidently did not have the patience for proper hunting strategy. Instead, he set all kinds of illegal traps in the woods for deer and smaller critters.

It was not every day one saw a six-pointer caught in a bear trap. Nor was it a pleasant sight.

Then there was the ever-growing issue of pollution. He had assisted in cleanup operations in wooded areas such as Rocky Mountain National Park. Large amounts of sulfur, emitted from a nearby power plant, traveled through the air into the park. As a result, lichens, a symbiotic combination of algae and fungi, grew on the trees, forming epiphytic microlichens. Growing on trunks of trees, they received their nutrients through the air. In the case of the southwest end of Rocky Mountain National Park, they served as the canary in the coal mine. Many different animals ate the lichens and used them for constructing nests, resulting in thousands of deaths.

Little by little, Julian found himself longing for the quiet, uneventful life of routinely patrolling the roads of Hesperia. He no longer craved 'adventure', nor did he feel a sense of purpose in his work. What good was it? The last three years was spent watching the literal decay of the environment at the hands of remorseless wrongdoers, and knowing it would continue no matter what he did. Every time he arrested somebody, they would either get released, or someone else would take their place. Maybe it was the fate of the world. Perhaps, this was humankind's legacy.

Whatever the case, hanging out at tackle shops did not sound so bad anymore.

When they arrived at port, he could already see Sheriff Baron Gillis standing on the pier. The *Lineman* was docked. Glenn was not the type to go easy on the throttle. Clearly, he wanted to beat Julian to the harbor so he could give his story first.

Lovely.

The Sheriff's Department did not take kindly to the young agent. It was unclear if they took offense to the EPA sending someone to investigate in their area, or if they hated outsiders in general. Whatever the reason, Julian was already dreading the upcoming conversation.

Sheriff Gillis was everything one would expect from a town like this: twenty pounds overweight, shirt wrinkly, face unshaven with two days' growth, and sporting a mustard stain on the left knee of his tan pants. Julian was shocked the guy bothered to tuck his shirt in.

But the small county kept reelecting him. Most of the population was cooped up in this gulf coast town of Pelican Grove. The rest of the county's inhabitants were suburban areas. Many of them only came there over the winter and returned to their northern properties in April. They often didn't bother voting in local elections. Thus, the county was practically owned by Pelican Grove.

The sheriff said something to Glenn, then stuck his hands in his pockets and watched Julian dock his boat.

"Sheriff!" Mark Wall exclaimed. "Just the man I want to see."

"Getting yourself into trouble, Mark?" Sheriff Gillis asked. It was more of a casual exchange of banter than a legitimate question. The way they spoke, it was obvious the two men had a history. Unfortunately for Julian, it was a friendly one.

"Just doing my business, then all of a sudden, this Clint Eastwood wannabe shows up out of nowhere. Threatened to draw his weapon and assault me with his stick thing."

Gillis glanced at Julian's baton then at his face. "That true, Mr. Reed?"

"That's *Agent* Reed," Julian replied. "And the fact of the matter is that Mr. Wall here was resisting arrest."

"Arrest?!" Gillis said with a belch. Its stench carried over to the helm of Julian's boat. "You have evidence of a crime?"

"Witnessed it myself. Mr. Wall was in the process of reeling in an illegal drift net. Been finding a lot of those around here, Sheriff. A lot of protected species travel through the Gulf. They are prone to getting snagged in these nets and killed."

"How do you know the net belonged to Mark Wall?" Gillis asked.

Julian pursed his lips.

Fuck my life. This cannot be happening right now.

He didn't hold the sheriff or his staff to any high standard, but this was too much. The sheriff was blatantly coming to Mark's defense. And Julian couldn't help but suspect Gillis was fully aware of the issues in their local waters, but couldn't give less of a shit. He was milking his way to retirement, munching on donuts and chili dogs to kill the time.

"Well, for starters, there's the dead shark on the deck of their boat." He pointed at the *Lineman*. "Not much nutritional value there. Even less legality."

"Oh, those," Gillis exclaimed. "Mark's first mate here was just now reporting the illegal drift net they came across. He brought these specimens to me as evidence of the criminal act."

Julian wanted to laugh. He wasn't sure which was more hilarious; the logic stretch, or the atrocious acting by the sheriff.

"Oh, is that so?"

"It certainly is, Agent. Looks like you arrested Mr. Wall by mistake. I'm willing to overlook this issue if you release him from custody right now. Or else, I will have no choice but to get in touch with your superiors."

Julian scoffed. "Go ahead."

"If you insist. I'm sure they'll be glad to learn how one of their agents is abusing his authority and harassing hard-working fishermen. A lot of drama has sparked up since you arrived, Agent. This is a quiet town. We like it that way. The mayor sees it that way too. If I remember correctly, he's friends with the congressman of our district, who's tight with the head of the EPA. Just food for thought."

Julian remained quiet for the next few moments. That desire to return home was stronger than ever. So strong in fact, he was giving thought to making a phone call to his old police chief. Maybe after getting back to his ratty hotel room. The EPA obviously didn't care too much about this assignment, or else they would have sent a whole team with him.

Apathy got the better of him. Julian pulled out his key and uncuffed Mark Wall. The snobby fisherman flashed a toothy smile of victory in the agent's face, then climbed onto the pier.

"Thank you, Sheriff. It's refreshing to know some law enforcement actually cares about the well-being of their citizens."

Julian shut his eyes. *Good sweet Jesus.* The act was painful to listen to.

"My pleasure, Mark," Gillis replied. "That's why I took the job."

This time, Julian snorted.

Gillis turned his eyes to the agent. "Something funny?"

Julian tied up the mooring lines, then stepped onto the pier. He started walking to shore, stopping momentarily as he passed the sheriff.

"Nothing at all."

With that said, he walked away, listening to their banter while he directed himself to the parking lot.

"So, how's the fiancée?" Gillis asked Mark.

"Makes a good martini, I know that much," Glenn chimed in.

"That's just the tip of the iceberg," Mark said. "As a matter of fact, I could use one right now. Except, I'm thinking bourbon."

Julian found his pickup truck and climbed into the cab. A slam of the door separated him from the conversation.

He sank in his seat and glanced at his smartphone. A quick Google search brought up images of his hometown. He saw a few lakes, including a little one called Butternut Lake where a local business had cottage rentals. He saw the local diner, Harlan's Heaven, where he often got coffee at the start of his shift. Then there was a screenshot of the small police and fire stations.

You don't know what you have until you lose it. Or, in my case, you don't know what you have until you give it up.

He clicked on the website link for the police station. Stan Tursten was still chief. As he scrolled down a list of staff, he saw some familiar faces. One of which was Deputy Tom Vance. He had to be nearing his sixty-fifth birthday by now, the age he had said he wanted to retire by.

There were one or two other guys who had to be close to retirement. If so, a few job openings would be on the horizon.

A wave of inspiration swept through the bitter agent. Maybe a phone call would be in order later today.

CHAPTER 4

When Mark Wall arrived at the Bait Bucket Bar and Grill, he got a hero's welcome from the crowd of patrons. That crowd was the usual lot of regulars, mainly fishermen and other residents in Pelican Grove. There was Gerry Grey, a shrimp fisherman and a third-generation resident of this coastal town. He was seated at a group of tables near Willy Phelps, Tony Bartram, Vic Millkie, Frank Mancuso, and a few others.

Nearly every afternoon and evening was spent draining glass bottles in this joint. The Bait Bucket was almost as old as Mark, though it had gone through a few different names during his lifetime, but only one remodel. The latest owner, Charlotte Pesko, had the longest tenure. It was probably due to her business model, which mostly consisted of: "If it ain't broke, don't fix it."

He caught a glimpse of the three-hundred-pound bay stater as she walked behind the bar. Having bartended for ten years up there, she decided she preferred the warm Florida weather as opposed to the freezing climate of the northeast coast.

It was a similar sentiment shared by the bartender.

Of all the familiar faces, hers stood out the most.

Mark Wall approached the counter, making sure to wave at the usual band of patrons huddling in the middle of the bar. Willy Phelps was telling some sort of stupid story. What it was, Mark couldn't care less. It was Willy Phelps. The story was almost guaranteed to be nonsense. Whatever the case, the other guys were amused by it.

He would catch up in a few minutes. First, he was interested in seeing his live-in girlfriend.

Maggie Pine brushed aside a few strands of brunette hair and offered a smile to her man. Mark took a seat and rested an elbow on the counter, eyeing the skull and flames sleeve tattoo that ran from her neck to her right elbow. The black tank top complemented the dark colors of the stripes and the orange tint of the flames.

"Take your break already?"

"I did," she replied.

"What a shame," he said. "Otherwise, I'd bring you to the backseat of my truck right this second." He clicked his tongue and smiled. The memories of their quickies were pleasant ones for him. Maggie was a woman who knew how to please, and rarely did she ever deny him his requests.

Today, she seemed less pleased with seeing him.

"What's the matter, baby?" he said. "Disappointed as I am?"

She leaned forward as to not be overheard by the others. "What happened today?"

"Hmm?"

"Out on the water. With the agent. What happened? I heard you were arrested."

Mark chuckled. It was pitiful she wanted to keep that between them, as if the others weren't already aware of it. Apparently, she wasn't aware of why they cheered his name when he entered the bar. Moreover, he found it hilarious that she was concerning herself with the issue.

"If you heard all of that, then obviously you know the sheriff acquitted me." He snapped his fingers and pointed at the bottle of Jack Daniels. "Fill me up, baby."

She pulled up a glass and poured the whiskey.

"But why?" she asked. "Why did the agent arrest you? What were you doing?"

Mark almost coughed the whiskey back up. "What makes you assume I was doing anything? I was working. I came across a net with some dead shark. Apparently, that triggered his little fee-fees and he decided to play tree hugger tough guy. What do you care?"

"Well…" She looked away, unsure if she wanted to express her concerns.

"Go on," Mark said. He finished his glass.

"You've been out a lot, lately. You've placed a lot of traps and drift nets in places that are pretty far out. And…" Maggie leaned forward again. This time, she absolutely wanted to keep from being overheard. "You've been bringing in a lot of money lately."

"You're complaining about that?"

She shook her head. "No, of course not. But let's be real, it's a little out of the ordinary. And abrupt. I assume your trap strategy is working, but I'm just worried it's adding risk. You could get caught and given a hefty fine. Or serve jail time."

Mark grinned and caressed her shoulder.

"I'll be fine. And if I'm caught, Gillis will back me up." He pushed his glass toward her. She took the hint and filled it. Knowing his tastes, she got him a Yuengling Black and Tan to go with it.

"Just be careful."

"You're not going to give me another lecture, are ya?" he said. "The bills don't pay themselves."

She smiled and shook her head.

Mark pulled out some cash and slapped it on the counter. "Maybe that'll ease your concerns. I'll give you the rest of your tip when you get home."

He clicked his tongue again, then left to join the other fishermen in the middle of the bar. An uproar of laughter piqued his interest. Everyone was spitting droplets of beer and doubling over—all except an embarrassed-looking Willy Phelps.

The pudgy, balding fisherman snatched his beer off the table and lifted it to his lips. "Laugh if you want, you bunch of pricks. But I'm telling you, that's what I saw."

He had a juvenile way of speaking, with each word having a slight drawl to it, as if the middle letter of each one somehow got snagged on his tongue on the way out.

"What'd you see?" Mark said, taking a seat next to the bearded Gerry Grey. "Apple pie? Elephant ear? Another woman repulsed by your face?"

The group laughed some more.

Willy belched and wiped his face. Usually, he was able to roll with the jokes. This time, however, he was red in the face, mad and humiliated all at once.

"No," Gerry said. "He claims he saw a sea monster."

"A big monster shark," Vic added. He mimicked some biting motions, then laughed some more.

Willy put his hands out. "I'm telling the truth."

Mark couldn't help but partake in the laughter. "Okay, Willie. Where'd you see it?"

"Three miles northwest of the lighthouse," Willy said. "Was out there hooking some shark late last night, making sure to avoid that agent fella."

The mention of that prick soured the taste of Mark's beer. He grimaced at the memory of his recent altercation, then forced it out of his mind.

"I was reeling in a nice eleven-footer. For once, this one was nice and healthy. Not sure what's been going on out there, but a lot of my catch has been shit lately. Like, seriously, haven't you noticed a bunch of them have been sickly, lately?"

His fellow fishermen nodded and murmured their agreement.

"Yeah," Tony Bartram said. "I trawled some tuna two days ago. Many of them were malnourished. Had to dump the catch. No good. Wasn't going to bother trying to sell it. The cannery would've offered pennies on the fish."

"Same," Gerry said. "Shrimping has been bad lately, too."

Mark waved a hand. "Alright, alright, alright. So the fishing's bad. Yeah, we've heard it all before. Give it a week or two, it'll be back to normal. I'm more interested in hearing about this monster shark Willy supposedly saw."

All eyes turned back to the captain of the *Round Five*. He bit his lip, unsure if he wanted to tell this story again. His alcohol-fueled need to convince them ultimately won him over, and he continued with the story.

"So, anyway, I was reeling in the shark, when all of a sudden the water parted like something out of the Bible. Then out of nowhere, this huge head comes up and grabs my shark and pulls it under the water." He paused, hoping for a proper reaction from his fellow drinkers, but only got blank stares of disbelief. "It's real! The thing chomped my shark down with one bite! It was huge!"

Mark crossed his boot over his knee and leaned back in his chair, winding his beer bottle in his hand.

"Late at night, you say?"

"That's right," Willy said.

Mark raised his beer. "And how many of these did you bring along?"

Again, the fishermen started laughing.

Willy sneered and sipped his own drink out of despair.

"It gets better," Vic said. "Hey, Willy. Tell us again what it looked like."

Willy groaned, not wanting to subject himself to their brutal heckling, but still desiring to prove himself right.

"This was no fever dream or drunken haze. The thing had big green eyes with slits like a cat's."

"Pupils," Mark said.

Willy waved him off. "Whatever. Its face was all messed up. There were big pores on its nose. Its skin was covered in some kind of slime, like it came out of a sewer or something. I don't know what it was. Sludge, maybe."

"I'd think the ocean would wash it away if that were the case," Mark said.

"I think it was secreting the stuff," Willy explained.

"Oh, secreting, huh?" Mark tried not to laugh, but failed.

"Laugh if you want," Willy said. "All I know is, if you guys saw what I saw, you'd be pissing your pants and going the other way."

"Kinda surprised that's what you did," Mark said. Willy perked up. "I mean, you have a shotgun, winch, and bait. I'm shocked you didn't try to catch and kill the thing. Hook it on a cable, bring it close to the boat, and put a couple shots in its head. Then you could tow it back home and prove to us you not only saw a monster shark, but *killed* it."

Willy stared into the distance. For once, he was unaffected by the chuckling from his peers. Inspiration struck, and all of a sudden, he was off his chair and heading for the door.

"That's exactly what I'm going to do! Hundred dollars says I'll bag that fucker by morning."

"I'll take that bet," Mark said.

"Me too," Vic added.

The other fishermen all voiced their willingness to partake in the bet.

Willy, pleased by this, removed his hat from a coat rack and went out the door. "See you shitheads in the morning."

"Night, Willy," Gerry said. He looked at Mark. "Oh, we shouldn't have done that. The douche won't be able to scrape enough cash together to pay us."

"He should've thought of that before he agreed," Mark said. He felt his phone buzzing against his hip. He unclipped the device and glanced at the screen. A wave of excitement struck as he read the name Ria Thorne, and the message *Meet now at your place?*

He typed back, *On my way,* then clipped the phone.

"Gotta go," he said. "Got some business to attend to." He finished his beer and whiskey, then left the glass on the table. He waved to Maggie, making sure to wink before heading out the door.

CHAPTER 5

Ria Thorne was leaning against his garage door when Mark pulled into the driveway. Her Buick Encore was still running, though its driver was outside. Clearly, she was hoping for a degree of anonymity in their meeting. Given her choice of clothing—jean shorts and a forest green crop top that was a size too small—*nobody* in this town would take notice of her face. With every meeting, it generally took Mark a few minutes before he made eye contact with her. Today was no different.

He used his remote to open the garage. Ria rewarded him with a glimmery white smile and a flick of her black hair before stepping into the Buick. She brought the vehicle into the garage, with Mark parking beside her. With another click of the remote, he shut the garage door and switched on the overhead lights.

"You came fast," Ria said. Immediately, she chuckled. "Of course, I'm referring to your response."

"Don't like keeping guests waiting," Mark replied. He crossed his arms and leaned against his truck, unsubtly admiring her figure. It was moments like this that made him reconsider the possibility of a god being real. If ever a woman had been perfectly crafted, it was Ria Thorne. And it was clear she wanted him to notice. Very clear. Such a figure standing before him in his property prompted one thought, or rather a question. "What do you want?"

Ria whipped her hair back again. "What's the matter? I can't dress appropriately for the Florida heat?"

"Sweetheart, reps like you *never* dress in a way to objectify themselves unless it's for gain," Mark said. "In your case, significant gain. I wasn't born yesterday, and it's not my first rodeo with you. What's the job?"

Ria stepped to the side to open her passenger door. "And here I was, thinking you liked what you were looking at."

"Didn't say anything to the contrary. I just occasionally think with my brain."

Ria pulled out a large briefcase, placed it on the hood of his truck, and opened it. Inside were several stacks of cash, with a yellow folder on top.

Mark took a moment to check out the down payment. “That’s twice as much as you paid me last time.” He opened the folder to look at the files. “Go figure.”

“Twice the pay, twice the load,” she replied.

“Twice the number of trips.” Mark shut the folder and faced Ria, with one elbow on the truck. “You do realize there’s an EPA agent in town. He’s snooping around, digging into everybody’s business. If I go pick up a bunch of barrels, he’s bound to notice.”

Ria cocked a half-grin. “You know we have that covered. We’ve proven that today, haven’t we.”

“What we’re talking about is different from drift netting. I get caught doing *this*, it might be something that’s outside the sheriff’s authority. He might not be able to get me off the hook.”

“Hmm.” Ria shrugged, then stepped forward to reach for the briefcase. “I’m a little disappointed. I thought you liked working with me. I guess I’ll have to find someone else who’s up to the task.”

“Good luck with that,” Mark said.

Ria snorted. “Good luck finding someone who wants to get paid? In this town? I’d have less luck in Mos Eisley. Though…” She ran her hand over his arm, then leaned in close, deliberately providing a direct view to her cleavage. “…I was hoping you’d say yes. Frankly, I’ve enjoyed our partnership.”

The tactic was working and Mark knew it. More importantly, *Ria* knew it.

He inhaled deeply through his nostrils, trying to maintain the image of a strong-willed, unwavering man. The stirring below his waistline, the rushing of blood, and the general excitement of doing something wrong was quickly overpowering him. Maggie had several more hours in her shift. More than enough time for him to ‘negotiate’ with Ria. What she didn’t know wouldn’t hurt her.

Deep down, he was laughing. Here he was, being offered more money than he knew what to do with, and yet he was more excited about this ‘bonus offer’ from the company rep.

Mark cleared his throat, trying to save face. “Is that right? Because I’ve saved you a bunch of money, right? I hear it costs big bucks to invest and maintain the infrastructure to properly dispose of all that shit.”

Ria’s lips were millimeters from his by now. “It very much does. The more you handle it for us, the more money we save. Therefore, the bigger bonus I get at the end of each quarter.”

“Ah-ha,” Mark exclaimed. “So, you’re just interested in me for the money. By that, I mean, the money you make thanks to me.”

Ria chuckled at his joke. “I like to think of it as mutually beneficial. That said, I’m very much enjoying the increase in my bank account. You’re not the only one with debts, you know? So, is there any additional way I can persuade you to do this job for me?”

She took his hand and placed it on her ass, nipping his chin as she did. Mark grinned. His game of ‘hard to get’ was reaching its end.

“Possibly.” He took advantage of her gesture and squeezed the goods. “What do you have in mind?”

“I can think of something.” With that said, she gently planted her lips on his. She followed it up with a wetter one, which Mark enthusiastically responded to. Her hands demonstrated her eagerness by undoing his belt buckle. “What do you say?”

Mark exhaled a moan of pleasure. “I suppose I can squeeze the job into my schedule.”

“Great! Let’s celebrate.”

She threw herself on him, locking her legs around his waist and dug her tongue into his throat. Mark went to the door and carried his mistress/business associate into the house and up the steps. The briefcase wasn’t going anywhere. He could retrieve it later.

For now, he had something more important to do. More accurately, some*one.*

***

Maggie counted the fifty cents the maggot Joe Lewy left on the counter. And a maggot he was, both in appearance and behavior. And eating habits. Four beers, two orders of mozzarella sticks, all the while ogling her with zero tact. She was used to serving pricks. The town was full of them, after all. But at least most of the others had the basic decency to leave a couple of bucks.

She wiped down the countertop as more patrons came in. Taking a moment to assess the new crowd, she groaned audibly.

If Joe Lewy wasn’t bad enough, there was Aiden Trench. He was a twenty-four-year-old high school dropout and obvious drug user with an aversion to toothpaste. His breath carried across the room, literally. The company he kept wasn’t much better.

From what she knew, the jerks did not work. The money they made was either from unemployment scams or doing things like bottle collecting. A more accurate expression for bottle collecting was ‘ransacking people’s recycle bins in nearby neighborhoods and taking the contents to a grocery store in Quincy, that had a recycling service’. Ten cents per bottle or can, times a few hundred was sometimes enough to buy a gram of heroin or cocaine. Or, in this case, buy some booze.

"Hey, bitch," Aiden said. "Give me a Budweiser and a bottle of Jim Beam Black."

Maggie glared at the moron and his friends.

Aiden shrugged and waited for his order to be met. "Did I stutter? The fuck is the holdup? Grab my drinks, lady."

One of his pals sat beside him and leaned over the counter to look at her rear. "Yep, just as I thought. Definitely a tight ass."

"In more ways than one," the other said.

Aiden laughed. "I can imagine." He proceeded to make kissing sounds at Maggie. "What? You put the merchandise on display and get offended when people take notice? Bitch, put the bottles on the counter."

Maggie drew a breath, suppressing the murderous urges within her. What was dying to be a expletive-filled rant came out as a calm, albeit growly tone.

"You even have the money to pay this time?"

Aiden put his fist on the counter. "The fuck you just say to me, woman?"

The rest of the patrons turned to watch, most of them amused by the drama that was rapidly unfolding. Par for the course in this town, none of them stepped in to be ready and assist with the disorderly customer, should he get violent. No, they just drank and watched.

"On three occasions, you were a dine and dash," Maggie said. "I'm not serving you unless you pay up front."

"Oh, is that right?" Aiden exclaimed.

The office door opened and out came Charlotte Pesko, her face red with ketchup from her snack and the rush of blood to her cheeks as her temper elevated to boiling point.

Without a moment's hesitation, she marched to Maggie. "The hell's going on out here?"

Maggie repressed a sigh. She knew there was no point in complaining about Aiden's behavior. If past experience taught her anything, it was that as long as it didn't escalate to physical violence, Charlotte couldn't care less about verbal abuse. As long as the customer paid, they could comment on the bartender all night long. With that in mind, Maggie had to lean on the fiscal issue rather than the behavioral.

"It's these guys again," she said. "They don't pay."

"Oh, is that right?" Aiden said. "Judging us by our appearances, are we?"

"No, just judging on past—"

Aiden pulled his wallet out and chucked a pair of twenty-dollar bills at her. "Call me a thief again. I dare ya. Do it, woman." He swiveled in his seat to look at Charlotte. “I suppose I’ll go somewhere else. I hear the Crow’s Nest doesn’t insult their customers.”

“No, that won’t be necessary,” Charlotte said. She reached for a phone at the end of the bar and dialed a number. “Hey, Lisa?... Yeah, it’s Charlotte. You mind coming in?... Terrific. Wanna be bumped up to full time? The hours are available…. Yeah, Maggie insulted some customers again.”

Maggie stepped back, mouth agape. She had no misconceptions about Charlotte being an angel, but for her to side with these assholes and out her in front of the entire bar? For a few bucks from a trio of guys with a reputation for stealing?

It took *everything* for Maggie not to bash the bottle of Jim Beam on the countertop. A monologue formed in her mind, but she had the self-awareness to know it was a waste of words. She walked to the back door to the kitchen and locker area and collected her items, then strutted to the exit.

Aiden and his worthless buddies waved to her. “Bye, bitch! Better luck on the street corner. I hear ol’ Duane Flowers will pay well for a blow—”

She slammed the door behind her, sparing herself from the completion of Aiden’s taunt. Continuing down the cracked parking lot, she found her ratty pickup truck.

Nearing one-hundred-and fifty miles, it was on its last leg. She started it up and cringed as the entire vehicle shook as though an entire rock band was playing inside the engine.

“God, I hate my life.” She grabbed her phone and gave thought to texting Mark. He wasn’t going to be pleased with the news of her firing. Then again, maybe he would be indifferent. He had been making a decent amount of money lately. Perhaps he would prefer having her around the house more.

Either way, she chose to break the news when she got home. She was struggling to figure out the wording for her text anyway. It was doomed to be a back-and-forth digital conversation anyway, even if she stated she would explain when she arrived home.

She pulled out of the lot for the last time and took a right.

For the entire trip, she remained silent. Her nerves were still rattled. The only solace was the imaginary theater of her punching Charlotte in the face and breaking a bottle over Aiden’s head.

Maggie pulled up into her driveway, then fumbled in her purse to find the remote control for the garage. She located it and pressed *open.*

The garage door slowly lifted.

Maggie squinted. To the right was Mark's pickup truck. Beside it was a newer vehicle; a black Buick Encore.

She sat there staring for a moment, during which her mind began putting the pieces together.

"No… He's not…"

She tried to come up with different rationalizations, none of which made sense. Most of Mark's friends parked in the road or on the driveway in front of the garage. On top of that, none of them drove a Buick Encore.

Maggie switched the engine off and entered the garage. First, she went to the Buick's passenger window and peeked inside. Sure enough, she saw some makeup materials and a woman's purse.

Her blood rushed. Questions arose. Who was this bitch? How long had this been going on? How many other women had Mark been fooling around with? What was the best method to kill him and get away with it?

She turned around to storm through the front door, only to stop at the sight of an open briefcase resting on top of Mark's truck. Inside were several blocks of cash. Hundred-dollar bills! A ton of them!

On top of the cash was a tan envelop. Curiosity got the better of Maggie. She opened it and glanced at the papers inside.

What she found was a list of chemical and physical materials and a number of barrels for each one.

Plastic wastes, chromium, oil, metal, DDT, radioactive sludge, petroleum distillates, phenol and cresol, formaldehyde, each one having at least a dozen barrels.

Maggie connected the dots in her mind.

"That son of a bitch."

She went through the door and stepped into the living room. Right away, she could hear the *thumps* through the ceiling. She made her way up the stairs, listening to the female voice moaning "Oh, yes. Yes!" in rhythm with each *thump*.

Maggie reached the top step and went into the hall. The bedroom door was open.

Might as well catch the bastard in the act and spare myself whatever lies and justifications he might contrive.

She stepped into the bedroom and crossed her arms.

There they were, deeply entrenched in their screwing that they didn't even notice an audience had arrived. Mark was on his back, breathing through his mouth, watching the form of the bitch riding him. She drove her pelvis down hard, her back arching and head tilted back, moaning her "oh, yes" with increased enthusiasm.

"Oh, yeah, baby," Mark whispered, his breathing rapidly increasing. Now, it was he who threw his head back. His fingers dug into the woman's legs as his entire body tensed.

The woman planted her arms behind her to keep her from reeling backwards as she let out a loud, pleasureful gasp.

Maggie could not believe what she was watching. She began to regret this tactic of catching Mark red-handed. She had never experienced such a fervent reaction from him. He was usually very quiet when giving in to her, aside from some heavy breathing. But this bitch looked like she was electrocuting him. And his reactions were not fake either. She could see the sweat glimmering from his forehead and chest. There was an excitement factor here that he was not getting from her.

For once, Maggie could not contain her instinctual reaction.

"What the fuck!"

Both parties turned their eyes to the spectator in the doorway. Mark's eyes widened again, this time out of surprise.

"Oh, Maggie… I, uh…"

"Please!" Maggie exclaimed. "Please say something like 'this isn't what you think'. PLEASE say it."

"What are you doing home? I thought you were closing at the bar?" he asked, still rubbing his hands on the woman's thighs as though it was a perfectly normal thing to do in front of his live-in girlfriend.

The brunette was still catching her breath, apparently unbothered to be caught butt naked by a complete stranger.

Maggie ran her hands over her face. This evening had been a colossal disaster. Not only did she lose her job, but also her boyfriend, and more importantly, a place to live. This was Mark's house. It was in his name only. Maggie may not have had much self-worth, but even she had enough self-respect to not stay here a minute longer after what she had just discovered.

The brunette peeled a few strands of sweat-soaked hair from her face. "This the Maggie you were telling me about?"

"Uh, yeah," Mark replied.

The woman smiled. "Pleasure to meet you. Did you learn a thing or two while you were standing there?"

"Yeah, most whores tend to be proud of their experience," Maggie retorted.

The woman proceeded to grind against Mark's manhood. "In this case, I very much am. You can stick around. Trust me, there's going to be more to watch. At least two more rounds."

Maggie couldn't believe what she was hearing. Her psyche was at its limit. She went for the closet and started grabbing all the clothes she could find. It was imperative she leave *now.*

"Just, fuck off."

The woman began to groan, proud to wave her sexual superiority in the face of Mark's old flame.

"Oh, I will. As a matter of fact…" She looked down at the results of her grinding and the pleasure on Mark's face. "Oh, big boy. You really are having a good evening. Set for more already, I see."

Maggie cupped her mouth following a dry-heave. This woman was a psycho. There was no other explanation. To be caught screwing around was one thing. But this woman was actually trying to fuck Mark in front of her. It was as though the change in circumstance excited her more.

She could hear the woman shift position to welcome Mark's manhood. That stupid 'oh, yes' filled the room again. Even worse, *Mark* was doing it now.

Maggie tensed. She held a few shirts in one hand and an empty briefcase taken from the top shelf in the other. Every vein in her arms, neck, and forehead bulged.

All sense of self control vanished in this individual split-second.

Maggie turned around and threw the briefcase across the room. Spiraling like a square-shaped frisbee, it soared over Mark's body, ultimately connecting one of its corners with the ridge of the woman's nose. She flung backward and hit the floor, legs kicking the air.

"YOU BITCH!!!"

"What the fuck, Maggie?!" Mark shouted.

Right then, Maggie felt the first ping of regret. Packing was out of the question. She had to leave this instant. The naked woman was already making her way to her feet. Her nose was bleeding from both the nasal cavities and the newly created gash, courtesy of the briefcase. The sight of blood added a demonic shade to her enraged face.

Part of Maggie wanted to partake in this fight. The more sensible part knew this could get even more out of hand. She was already at risk of facing jailtime as it was.

Maggie sprinted through the door and flew down the stairs. All the while, the woman continued yelling obscenities and threats at her. It was practically an exorcist scene, with the pain and blood adding a growly texture to her voice.

Maggie made her way outside and got in her truck.

"Please start."

Fortunately, it did, though not without its nerve-wracking shake. She backed out of the driveway and sped down the road, abandoning all of her possessions.

A series of foul words left her mouth. This day had been absolute shit. And it wasn't over yet. She had nowhere to sleep.

"I hate my life," she said. There was nobody to call. There were no friends in this town worthwhile. She had very little money. At the same time, she wasn't willing to resign herself to sleeping in her truck just yet.

She stopped at a red light and took a breath. Slowly but truly, her heart rate slowed and her mind calmed. Once the light was green again, she was ready to start figuring out short-term solutions.

It was getting dark and she was tired as hell. A hotel was in order. Luckily, she knew of a cheap one.

At least one thing was going in her favor.

CHAPTER 6

Maggie arrived at the Ten Feathers Hotel. Located in the center of town, it was as ratty as the rest of Pelican Grove. Its name came from its humble beginnings. Before it became a two-story building with forty rooms, it was a small motel with ten rooms. Ten feathers of the pelican, its original owner rationalized. Maggie didn't think the phrase had as good a ring as he did. Nobody did. But the place was serviceable, built at a time when Pelican Grove had hope of being a lively town with economic success.

Eventually, the owner saw the writing on the wall with this town. Seeing that tourism was favoring pretty much every part of Florida but here, he sold the business and moved to a place near Palm Beach.

Maggie parked her truck and sat quietly, looking at the T and the N of the neon sign 'Ten Feathers'. The E was dark, its LED having died out a few months back. The current manager never bothered to replace it and nobody around here ever seemed to care. It wasn't a place admired for its aesthetics. A good majority of its patrons were married people coming from out of town to get busy without their spouses finding out.

Her adrenaline was finally starting to dwindle. The memory of recent events replayed in her mind over and over, fueling concern over retaliation. After all, she did hit that woman in the face with the corner of a briefcase. She and Mark were probably burning all of her belongings at this very moment.

Maggie was still uncertain about what she would do in the long run. She had no job, no prospects for future employment, no home, and soon—judging by the way her truck was rumbling—no vehicle.

"Dwelling on this will do no good," she told herself. "Worry in the morning. For now, get a fifth of bourbon from the liquor store down the street, a shower, and eleven hours of sleep."

She walked into the front lobby. At the desk was a scrawny man in his late thirties, with a wiry beard, most of which was on his neck, and a long hairstyle that definitely did not suit him. He was leaning on his elbow, sniggering at something on his computer monitor. He didn't take notice of Maggie until she tapped the bell on the countertop.

"Hello?"

The guy begrudgingly paused his video and swiveled in his seat to face her. "Can I help you?"

Maggie closed her eyes and tightened her lips. *No. I thought I'd just step in this building for fun.*

"Yes. Are there any rooms available?"

"You have a reservation?"

Maggie waited a moment before answering, quelling the instinct to make a snide remark on this guy's obvious stupidity.

"No." *Hence I asked if there are any FUCKING ROOMS AVAILABLE!*

The guy rolled back to his computer. "Okay, let's see what I have here. I have standard rooms with regular double beds, a king's suite with a hot tub and king-sized bed… hot tub doesn't work, though…"

"A standard will do just fine," Maggie said.

"Okay. I just need to borrow your driver's license and debit card, and I'll have you all set. It's one-thirty a night, with a seventy-dollar security deposit."

Maggie handed over her driver's license, waited for the guy to punch in the information he needed, then handed him the debit card.

He swiped it.

Beep!

"Hmm." He swiped it again.

Beep!

Shrugging, he handed it back to her. "Declined."

"Huh?" Maggie took the card back and looked it over, making sure it was the correct one and not her nearly maxed-out Capital One credit card. "I don't understand…" She wiped the chip clean then handed it back. "Try one more time please?"

He did.

Beep!

"Sorry."

Maggie took the card back and dug her phone out. *This can't be happening right now!*

"Okay, just, um, hold on a second." She got on her banking app to check her funds. "What the fuck?! That bastard!"

She always had mixed feelings about linking bank accounts with Mark. Today, her paranoia was confirmed. The bastard took all the funds from her checking and savings and transferred it to his own account. His next action was to block her access to his accounts, preventing her from taking the money back. Clearly a retaliatory move, probably on the behest of that woman he was shanking in bed.

Whatever the reason, it was an effective action nonetheless. Maggie was as broke as the drugged out, homeless people begging on the street corner a couple of blocks west.

The clerk extended her license back to her. "If you can't pay, there's not much I can do for you." He eyed her figure. "I mean…"

"Not in your wildest dreams." She snatched the card from his fingers and turned around, now feeling twice as disgusted. More than ever, she wanted to leave this cesspool of a town. Being poorly educated and prone to making poor decisions, mainly in men, she found herself unable to escape. That, and Pelican Grove was really the only place she ever knew. The thought of travel gave her anxiety. Plus, there was the fear of ending up somewhere even more crummy. Ultimately, it came down to favoring the devil she knew versus the devil she didn't know.

And the devil she knew was really kicking her ass right now. She exited the hotel, cursing with each step. She stopped at the end of the porch and looked at the functioning street lights, uncertain of what to do or where to go. Her eyes settled on her truck. Just the sight of that bucket of bolts elevated her anxiety. It was a disaster waiting to happen. Sure, it was all paid off, but what good would that do when it was on the verge of breaking down?

She fumbled through her wallet. Forty bucks was all she had to keep herself afloat. It was all she had. Thanks to taking the bait back at the house, she didn't even have a change of clothes.

"I'm fucked."

A pair of headlights entered the parking lot. It was a large, white truck with the label Environmental Protection Agency printed on the side.

The agent! I heard about him.

Word spread fast in Pelican Grove, especially in bars. There, she overheard the customers talking about the EPA agent trying to bust people for trapping, and that he claimed there were some toxicity levels in the water.

Her mind went to the briefcase and the tan folder on Mark's truck.

A new wave of adrenaline surged through her veins. Instead of anger and anxiety, this one was from joy. What better way to retaliate against that dickhead Mark Wall than to rat out his new business to someone who could put him in jail.

The door opened and out stepped the agent. He was just under six feet, well built, dressed in a white t-shirt tucked into some jeans. In his hand was a bag of takeout with the label Tractor Trailer. It was a joint located a few miles out of town.

Hmm.

Already, she liked what she saw. Not only was this agent good-looking, but he also had brains, considering he knew not to get food from this part of town. The locals had a tolerance for the low quality. Out-of-towners often left with cramps.

Maggie quickly brushed her hair back, sported a smile, then waved at the agent.

"Hey!"

"Oh, no. Not another one." Julian Reed had seen the woman standing in front of the hotel entrance when he pulled into the driveway. It was bad enough that every night he had to listen to the thumping from the rooms adjacent to his. Of course, the agency booked a place that was as clean as a Russian prison block. First night, two hookers offered their services as he brought his luggage into the building. Last night, he had the misfortune of walking past a vehicle in the lot, where a fella was getting 'serviced'.

He gripped his takeout bag tightly, then started veering to the right to avoid her. The woman was maybe in her late twenties, sporting a sleeve tattoo that ran from her shoulder to her right wrist. Her attention was definitely on him.

"No thanks. Have a nice night."

"Wait, hold on. You're the agent, yes?"

Julian weaved around the woman. They all asked that question, probably because they thought feigning admiration for his job and authority would increase his likelihood of purchase.

"Yes. Again, no thanks. Not interested."

She turned to follow him, nearly tripping over her own feet. "There's something I have that you want. *Need.* It'll make your job easier."

Julian chuckled. This one was really eager.

"Sorry. It's dinner time."

"Well, if you're willing, I could join you in your room. We can—"

Julian turned around and held his hand out, stopping the woman in her tracks. She threw her arms out to catch her balance, shocked by his sudden aggression.

"Ma'am, the answer's no. If you're that eager to earn some quick cash, I guarantee you the clerk will gladly take you up. While he's on the job. I couldn't care less."

The woman's face shriveled up, all at once dumbfounded and pissed. Julian braced for the storm. Most hookers threw a few curse words and insults when rejected, but this woman? She looked like a volcano ready to erupt.

"Back the truck up!" she said. "Are you calling me a whore?"

Julian stepped back. "Well…" he couldn't think of what to say, eventually settling with, "Aren't you?"

She didn't need to answer. He knew as soon as the words left his mouth.

Oh. Whoops.

The woman turned her back to him. He noticed how her hand briefly raised over her shoulder, only to drop to her side. She had a mind to slap him, but reconsidered.

"You know what? Never mind. Go and stuff your sorry ass with that junk. Sorry I bothered you." She started walking toward a crummy-looking pickup truck that looked like it was being held together with spit and glue.

Julian groaned, then followed her. "Excuse me. Ma'am?" The woman stopped and turned, burning him with a glare. Julian stopped, watching those eyes as though they may spit fire at any moment. "M-my apologies. I thought you were trying to, uh… I thought you were, um…"

"A hooker?"

"Mm… maybe more like a…uh," He cleared his throat. "Yeah." An awkward silence passed for a few moments, during which they idly stared at one another. "So! Considering I know better, what can I help you with?"

The woman took a breath and cooled down. Her shoulders unhunched and her posture became more relaxed. Her smile returned, joined by a nervous laugh. She broke eye contact as she thought back on their encounter.

"Damn, I'm sorry. To say it's been a shitty day is an understatement. A really big understatement. Like, one for the ages. I'm just now realizing how I came off, standing there, in this part of town…" She took a breath, taking in a whiff of the aroma coming out of Julian's takeout bag. "By the way, on a sidenote, that place is the bomb. When I referred to it as junk, that was the "I was just called a hooker" anger talking." She laughed anxiously, only to realize she was still staring at the bag like a dog eyeing a bone. Embarrassed, she tapped herself on the cheek to refocus her mind. "I guess for starters, I should introduce myself. I'm Maggie."

"Agent Julian Reed. You said there's something about my job? You offering a tip?"

"More than a tip," Maggie said. "You're checking for toxic spills, right?"

"That's right," Julian said.

"I know something about it." Her eyes went to the takeout bag again. "I…"

Amused, Julian glanced at the bag. "Food's good, but I don't think it's *so good* that it warps your mind. Unless you count the carb coma."

"No, I'm sorry. Again, long day. Haven't eaten since noon. Been busy ever since, then ran into some problems just a short while ago…"

Julian noticed the subtle tremors. He knew exactly what they were. Jitters from low blood sugar and possibly some anxiety. From what he could see, she wasn't on drugs. Pupils were not dilated, no needle marks, no drying around the nose or mouth, as well as numerous other symptoms. No, this was just a hungry and nervous woman who appeared to be in a lot of trouble.

"Are you okay?"

"Yes," Maggie said. Her fake smile quickly withered. "No. I just lost my job, got kicked out of my place, discovered my live-in boyfriend in bed with some hoe, my truck's a piece of junk, and I have no money."

Julian gulped. "All in one night?"

"All in one night."

He bit his lip, feeling his compassionate side starting to kick in. It would probably appear unethical, but he knew the truth of his intentions. At worst, if anyone noticed, they would brush it off as a hookup. All in all, he did not want to remain standing outside in this parking lot at night.

"Listen, I ordered too much. I tend to think with my stomach when I order out. End up having leftovers for lunch and dinner the next day. If you're comfortable, you can come up to my hotel room, eat something, and discuss what you know. Is that alright?"

Maggie smiled. "Oh, you don't have to do that, Agent sir. I should've known better than to stare at your dinner."

"Nah, it's perfectly fine."

Her stomach growled loudly, prompting a laugh from both of them. Maggie nodded and walked with him to the hotel. As they expected, they got a grin from the clerk as they walked past the counter to the stairway. Not that he cared. He was too busy watching porn on his computer.

Julian shook his head.

This town, I swear.

CHAPTER 7

"Oh, dear God. This is the one good thing to happen to me today," Maggie said. She finished her inhalation of Julian's spare burger and fries, then leaned back in her chair.

Julian had only gotten through a couple bites of his. The poor woman must have been starving. He sat at the other end of the small dining table and checked his phone. It was going on eleven. He let Maggie eat before pressuring her about her info on the dioxin levels. She was clearly stressed back in the parking lot, and based on training and experience, it was best to interview people when they had a few minutes to calm down first. Otherwise, details got jumbled.

"I take it you're feeling better."

"Oh, yes." Maggie closed her eyes and cringed, still embarrassed. "Listen, Agent…"

"You can just call me Julian."

"Julian, thanks again for this. I don't want to give the impression that I'm some freeloader who takes food from complete strangers and hangs out with them in shady hotel rooms. You'll find plenty of those in this town. Not me. It's just that I've…"

"Had a rough night," he said, completing her thought.

"Yes."

"Let's start with your situation," Julian said. "You said you got kicked out of your house?"

"It was my boyfriend's house. *Ex*-boyfriend," Maggie replied. "Right after I got fired from the bar I worked at. Apparently, my boss is fine with repeat dine-and-dashers coming in, because 'maybe' this time they might actually pay. Ugh." She waved her hand to dismiss the topic. "So, I come home, find another vehicle in the garage. Lo and behold, he's in bed getting ridden by this chick. There might've been an…" she cleared her throat and shifted her eyes, "an altercation of sorts."

Julian read between the lines. "Let me guess. It got physical."

"Am I under oath?"

Julian chuckled at that. "How bad did it get?"

"I might've thrown something at her and knocked her off the bed," Maggie said. "Nothing she won't walk away from, if that's what you mean by 'bad'."

Julian gave a comforting smile. It was all he wanted to know regarding that incident. He wasn't going to waste his time reporting this woman for a little scuffle unless it resulted in significant bodily injury. Maggie was having a bad enough day as it was. And, as far as he was concerned, if you're caught hooking up with someone's partner, you're due a right hook or two. That was a personal opinion rather than a professional one.

"Probably best to keep that information on the down low," he said. "What about money?"

"Don't have any," Maggie said. "Didn't have much to begin with, but now I'm broke except for the cash in my wallet. You see, in addition to being stupid enough to shack up with Mark, I was dumb enough to link my bank accounts with him. Basically, we went all the way when playing house. I actually wish I married him so I could drag his ass through the legal system."

"Hang on," Julian said. "You linked accounts. Are you implying he drained all of your money?"

Maggie bit her lip and nodded. "I don't suppose I can get it back…"

"Ehh." Julian gritted his teeth. "I mean, *technically* it's possible, but when you combine accounts like that, it gets tricky to prove theft."

"Yeah, that's what I thought," Maggie said. "So, yeah, I'm on the streets now, taking food from strangers. Hell, I'm only a couple hours out, and I was already mistaken for a hooker." She started to laugh at that, only for a somber look to come over her face. "At this rate, I'm worried I might actually stoop to that level at some point."

"You'll find a job," Julian said. "You're clearly smart and have some level of self-respect. You'll be fine."

Maggie sported a grin, though still feeling down in the dumps. "I appreciate it."

Julian tapped his fingers on the table, waiting as a few moments of silence went by. "So… aside from circumstance, what made you want to come talk to me?"

All of a sudden, Maggie perked up.

"Something that'll help us both," she said. "It'll help you with your job and grant me a little sweet revenge."

Julian leaned forward, hands cupped on the table. "I'm listening."

"Lately, Mark's been bringing in more money," she explained. "He'd been in debt for a while. Fishing hadn't been working out too well lately. But all that changed when he took a new job. He never really explained what it was, and I never asked, since I was busy with my own problems. Plus, he never really liked talking about work. Even when I joined him on his fishing trips, he never seemed too enthused."

"Hold on a sec," Julian said. "Mark… fishing… Mind telling me Mark's last name?"

"Wall. Mark Wall," Maggie said.

"You were living with Mark Wall?!" Julian asked.

"I suppose you know him," Maggie said. "I've heard him say a few, how should I put it? Unkind things about you. Including at the bar today. He visited me before shit hit the fan."

"Yeah, I caught him red-handed with an illegal drift net," Julian said. "Sheriff decided to let him off."

"Sheriff Gillis? Yeah. He grew up with these people. Pretty much cut from the same cloth. He pretty much runs this place. Unless someone does something seriously bad, like murdering someone, none of these townspeople are going to jail. And even then, I'd be surprised in some cases, to be honest."

"You think Mark has something to do with the dioxin levels I'm finding in these local waters?" Julian asked.

"I know he is," Maggie said. "When I got home, I found a briefcase full of cash, and a manifest of what looked like chemical waste to be disposed of. My guess is that lady he's hooking up with is part of some company. The briefcase was in the garage. My guess is that they were discussing business there before going upstairs to seal the deal."

"Pretty reasonable assessment," Julian said. "Do you have the manifest with you?"

Maggie scratched her head. "Yeeaaah… no. I kind of left in a hurry, following the incident."

Julian sighed. For a moment, he was sure he would have a shortcut to finishing this case. He had been on the phone with his old police chief in Hesperia. At the start of their phone conversation, the chief jokingly asked "how are things? Missing the old town?" Julian took advantage of that opening, replying "A little bit, yes. Actually, more than a little bit, to be honest." To his relief, the chief read between the lines and mentioned how a few positions would be opening soon. By the end of the chat, Julian found himself feeling uplifted.

There was one condition to the chief's proposal: *"Solve your case. Do not quit. EARN the job."*

It was the motivation he needed to keep moving forward here in Pelican Grove.

"Do you remember what was on the manifest?" he asked.

"There were a lot of things," she said. She shut her eyes and tried to remember. "Plastic wastes, oil, formality… I mean formal, uh, formy-something…"

"Formaldehyde?"

"I think that was it," Maggie said. "Let's see, there were others. I only took a quick look at the thing. Damn, I should've taken a photograph with my phone. There was something about radioactive waste. Petroleum-something… second word began with a 'D'."

"Probably petroleum distillates," Julian said. "It's a complex bond of hydrocarbons. People and animals exposed to them can get cancer."

"Damn," she muttered. "There was other stuff, but I can't remember all of it."

"It's alright," Julian said. "I get the picture. What about locations?"

"That part's up in the air," Maggie said. "Can't you arrest Mark and interrogate him? I mean, I provided evidence of his involvement. There's probable cause."

"If you brought me the manifest, then yes, that would be the case. Here's the problem," Mark explained. "You're an ex-girlfriend who, justifiably, is holding a grudge. On a human level, I totally get it. Legally, a judge would laugh me out of the courthouse if I tried to get a warrant based on your word alone. Plus, given what you told me of what went down at the house, it might come back to bite you."

Maggie rested her head on her palm. "Fair enough." She thought for a moment then sat up straight. "Hang on, I've been out on the water with him. I know where his usual fishing grounds are. Some of them go out pretty far, but I remember where they are."

"He would contaminate his own fishing grounds?" Julian asked. "Sounds like he'd be shooting himself in the foot."

"Not for the amount of money he's getting paid," Maggie said.

Julian stood up to go to his dresser drawer. He pulled out a white three-ring binder and started flipping through some pages, eventually finding a paper map of the bay.

"Any of these areas look familiar?"

Maggie studied the small map. "Yeah, but there's only a couple areas here where he fishes. Most go farther out."

"Makes sense," Julian said. "He'd probably want to sink the stuff in deeper waters. Do any of these places have names?"

"Not really," Maggie said. "There's a spot near Jefferson Island he goes near, and sometimes he fishes over the Rastro de Lágrimas Canyon. It's a pretty big area several miles out. The only spot on this map where Mark fishes is right here." She put her finger on the westernmost edge of the paper. "Sometimes he trawls here, a mile or so north of a channel marker floating in the area."

"Perfect! At least I have something to work with." Julian moved to the closet and pulled out a jacket.

Maggie tilted her head. "You going out?"

"Might as well. Sooner I find the dumping grounds, the sooner I'm out of this godforsaken town," Julian said.

"Can't begrudge you for that sentiment," Maggie said. "Are you gonna be able to navigate in the dark? You even know which way you're going?"

"I have a map," he said.

"You don't even know where the channel marker is," Maggie said. "Not for the other places. You're not gonna find squat unless you have someone who knows the local waters."

Julian stood by the edge of the bed, badge and duty belt in hand. He tried to think of an argument against her point, only to come up with nothing. Furthermore, he was able to read between the lines.

"You offering to come with me?"

Maggie shrugged. "Why not? I've got nowhere to be. I'm used to closing down bar at two in the morning, and taking another half-hour to clean up. I'm usually not in bed until three-thirty at best."

Julian considered her offer. Being an overthinker, he worried about appearances. Man and a woman, alone on a boat late at night, would probably garner certain assumptions by anyone who saw them together. Then again, he'd already brought her up to his hotel room.

Most importantly, he realized there was one thing he cared about more than appearances. That was getting this damn job done and over with. If Maggie could help him find Mark's dumping grounds tonight, then he'd be out of here in a couple of days. Maybe he would take part in the ensuing investigation, maybe get to participate in the arrest of the perpetrator, and once it was over, he'd return to his hometown with a 'war story' to tell.

"Alright, then. Let's go."

Maggie stood up. "Hate to sound like an entitled bitch, but is there any chance of bringing refreshments? It's bound to be a long trip."

"We'll stop somewhere on the way. Then again, the only places still open are liquor stores."

Maggie grinned. "Works for me."

CHAPTER 8

Julian was quickly regretting his choice to conduct his search at night. Despite his regular intake of coffee, his natural sleep clock was ticking hard. His eyes threatened to shut against his will, forcing him to take extra precautions while performing tests on the water.

Maggie was seated on the flying bridge, visibly bored with a soda bottle dangling from her fingertips. When she asked for refreshments, she was hoping for something more in line with tequila. Julian was already feeling slightly uncomfortable being alone with a woman he just met. Allowing her to get intoxicated would only complicate matters further. Especially considering she was fresh from a rotten breakup and was eager to get back at her ex.

The past ninety minutes were spent with idle chit-chat. Julian got to learn more about Mark Wall… more than he cared to know, in some aspects. Maggie was a bit more civilized than most people he had met in Pelican Grove, but she still lacked tact. Some of the knowledge was insightful, even if predictable. Mark Wall was a gambling addict with a lot of debts. Shocker! Six years ago, he served four months in jail for assault after an altercation in the parking lot of some chain restaurant out of town.

Maggie also had knowledge about Mark's fishing mate, Glenn. That information proved a little more worrisome. The guy was a veteran of the Iraq War and was given a general discharge after thirty months and two tours of service—the second of which was cut short. The reason: the guy had 'accidentally' gunned down the cousins of a sniper they were tracking. They had tracked the target to a building. Glenn claimed he got a visual and opened fire. Instead of the target, he cut down two civilians.

Some witnesses indicated the family members were trying to signal for help. One of the soldiers testified that the casualties were in plain sight through the window and were clearly not a threat. Other soldiers, possibly due to bias, simply testified that they did not see the civilians before Glenn shot them, therefore they could not attest whether he shot them on purpose or not.

According to Maggie, the tactic worked. The deaths of his cousins got the sniper to engage and get sloppy with his tactics, making his location known. It wasn't long before the squad of soldiers were able to take him down. The situation was investigated, Glenn was court martialed, and ultimately let go. Due to insufficient evidence of malice, and given his service record, which included a purple heart, he was not given a dishonorable discharge, but a general.

Ultimately, Glenn bluntly told Mark he knew the people he killed were cousins, and laughed about it.

This new bit of info made Julian think twice about exposing Mark Wall's involvement in the pollution of the local waters. If Mark was involved, it was safe to assume that Glenn guy was too. Given his history, it stood to reason that Glenn would be more than happy to go to extreme measures to stay out of prison.

This new feeling of anxiety, in addition to sleepiness, made Julian consider heading back to shore. Maybe he would just call it quits and return to Hesperia. Sure, it wasn't the most ethical of decisions, but apathy was a powerful drug.

Julian finished the water test with his kit.

"Anything?" Maggie asked.

"Nothing," he replied. "Well, not nothing. There are traces of dioxin, but they're faint. Just like everywhere else I've tested."

"You gonna send your drone into the water again?" She pointed at the

orange and black Jerico underwater drone that rested by the transom. The device was equipped with cameras fore and aft, and was capable of descending to depths up to four-hundred-and-ninety feet. It was his primary tool for combing the ocean bottom.

Unfortunately, it was borderline useless, not because the drone was no good, but the scope of the search area. This entire search was practically a needle in a haystack.

It was all the more reason why Julian was fed up with his career with the EPA.

"I don't think so," he said. "There's no point. The stuff's not here." He looked to the dark horizon. "It's somewhere out there, though."

He kept his gaze on the moonlit water, watching the stars reflecting on the glassy surface.

Maggie hung her head to the side and exhaled through her lips. There was nothing to do except stare. Like Julian, she regretted coming out here, but then again, she had nowhere to go.

"I guess we'll head west," he said. He secured his test kit and climbed to the flying bridge. Maggie got out of the chair and let him take over.

"Bet you're wishing you brought some beer out here now, aren't ya?"

He shook his head. “No. I don’t drink much these days. Besides, it’d probably make me pass out over the wheel.” He demonstrated his point with a drawn-out yawn.

Maggie leaned against the rail. “You don’t drink, huh? Is it a discipline thing or you just don’t like the taste?” She smirked. For a second, she considered making a jab at him about being the kind of guy that only liked fruity drinks.

A scowl took form after the answer came to light.

“No. My dad was killed by a drunk driver,” he said.

Maggie cringed. “Oh…” She facepalmed. “Sorry. Wasn’t expecting that.”

“Nah, it’s alright,” he said. “Happened back in my teens. He worked late, was on his way home, some idiot ran a red. Unfortunately, it’s not a unique story, but true all the same.”

Maggie glanced at the Dr. Pepper in her hand. All of a sudden, she wasn’t looking at it while wishing it would turn into a bottle of bourbon.

“You have parents?” Julian asked.

“Ha!” She shrugged and made a goofy facial expression. “Mom died of a drug overdose when I was fourteen. Dad left a little before that. Skipped town with some whore.”

“Oh.” Julian wasn’t sure what else to say.

“They didn’t stay together. Dad was hardly in the picture, and Mom was too busy wrecking her life,” Maggie continued. “I was pretty much on my own from then on. The government tried to hook me up in some foster care program. Let’s just say, I never showed up. After a while, they gave up.”

Julian kept the boat pointed west and cruising at ten knots. By the looks of it, they had the entire Gulf to themselves, save for one boat a half-mile to the northwest.

He turned in his seat to look at Maggie. “You ever finish high school or get your GED?”

She shook her head. “What good would it have done me?”

“Well…” Julian nodded toward the harbor lights that illuminated the edge of Pelican Grove. “It would make it easier to get out of this place.”

“Yeahhhh.” Maggie’s voice was long and drawn out. “If only I considered that back then. I’m stuck here now. I suppose you’re right, though. I should’ve made better decisions and got myself a lucrative career like you did. Then I wouldn’t be in this mess.”

Julian shrugged. “Careers are sometimes overrated.”

“Say that when you’re in my shoes,” Maggie replied. She took a breath and gave new thought to Julian’s statement. “You not like your job?”

"Kind of hit a burnout state," Julian said.

"Really?"

"Yeah. After a while, you realize you're not really making a difference. You get sick of the red tape, dealing with assholes on a daily basis, the constant traveling…"

"Hmm. I thought traveling would be the best part of the job," Maggie said.

"Not when it's always to places like this," Julian said. "When all you see is degradation of the ecosystem. I don't consider myself an environmentalist. I like steak and fish as much as the next guy, and I'm not gonna throw a fit every time a tree gets cut down. But when you see the effects of chemicals on multiple acres of land, or see miles of contaminated water and dead fish, you start to lose a little faith in humanity."

Maggie looked at the water. "I guess that makes sense. I guess I never really thought much about it. My mind's usually set on making it to the next paycheck." She drained the last of her bottle and placed it on the deck, making sure not to accidentally drop it in the water in front of the agent. "So, what's your plan? Gonna stay with the EPA?"

Julian cupped his hands and rested them behind his head. "Fortunately, this is shaping up to be my last assignment. I spoke with my old boss earlier today and it looks like I have a good shot at getting my old job back."

"Yeah? Where?"

"My hometown. Little place in Kansas you've never heard of. Lots of trees, country folk, plenty of rivers and ponds for fishing. It has its own little police department. I worked there for a few years before moving on to what I thought would be bigger and better things."

"Oh. Interesting." Maggie struggled to feign enthusiasm for his decision. "Sorry. I guess that sounds really boring. No offense."

"None taken."

"I mean, that place sounds nice for a getaway," she continued. "But, I don't know, I think I'd go crazy living in the same tiny place, seeing the same ol' people… I guess I should know. I've lived in this dump all my life. I guess one advantage of your town is that the residents are probably not bottom dwellers."

Julian snorted. "That they are not. Just people who like peace and quiet. Sometimes you get people who like to take their boats out at night for fishing trips. Kinda like this guy." He pointed his thumb at the boat in their vicinity.

Maggie tilted her head to look at it.

She squinted, then stood up straight for a better view.

Seeing the stern expression on her face, Julian quickly turned to look at the boat.

"What the hell?"

He slowed the boat down and began turning to starboard.

The vessel was tilting on its starboard quarter, the underside visible beneath its partly raised bow.

Julian pointed at a spotlight near Maggie. "Hey, can you turn that on and point it?"

Maggie did so. A large white stream touched the oddly positioned vessel. She sucked in a deep breath, seeing the indentations on its underside. Tilting the light up a few feet, she panned over the portside gunwale. There were two sections along the aft deck where the side had been caved in, as though a torpedo-shaped force had connected with the vessel.

She swung the light leftward and held it on the words *Fifth Round,* printed on the bow.

"Oh, my God. That's Willy Phelps' boat."

"I take it you know who that is?" Julian asked.

"He's a fisherman. I saw him earlier today at the bar," Maggie said. She swept the light over the vessel. The windshield glass on the pilothouse was shattered.

Even more bizarre was the flying deck. The portside corner was gone. At first glance, it seemed to have broken away from the same type of collisions that wrecked the hull. Yet, Julian could not take his eyes off it. The edges of the 'indentation' appeared chiseled and discolored, the metal frame exposed and also deteriorated.

As though it were melted.

His hand instinctively rested on his sidearm.

"What the hell happened?"

"Should we call the sheriff?" Maggie asked. "I know your opinion of him. But still…"

"We will, but I wanna take a look at something first," Julian said. He brought their boat around the bow and lined up with the *Fifth Round's* starboard side. With the boat on a slant, they were able to look directly at the deck.

Maggie moved the light to the *Fifth Round's* aft section. Scattered across the partly flooded deck was Willy's fishing gear. A large rod had been set up. Floating in the water were severed shark fins.

"Looks like Willy Phelps was doing a particular kind of fishing," Julian said.

"He was talking up a storm at the bar," Maggie said. "Something about some God-awful shark he saw while fishing last night. The guys laughed his story off and dared him to go catch it."

"They won't be laughing this one off," Julian replied.

Maggie held the light on Willy's fishing rod. The pole was leaning against the gunnel, its fishing line extended into the water.

Julian brought the vessel as close to the other as possible. "Here, take the wheel." He let Maggie take his place, then carefully crossed over onto Willy's boat.

Already, he felt gravity threatening to pull him down the slope into the water. He made his way to the pilothouse, taking notice of strange little burns on the side of the structure and on the deck. And there was no doubt they were burns, and not ones made by fire. Whatever did this, it was liquid and corrosive. He had seen it during his training and had personally seen such acids, or rather their aftermath, during an investigation of a chemical spill in California. That particular instance was the result of moronic college-age psychos thinking they were being edgy by uploading animal abuse videos to the dark web.

But this? This was something else.

He opened the door into the pilothouse. "Mr. Phelps? Are you here?"

The pilothouse was empty.

Farther into the structure was a single room comprising the cabin and mess hall.

Julian opened the door, finding a small empty bunk and a little dining table. The overhead light had been left on, the cabinets were open, and the dishes had fallen out and shattered all over the floor.

When he returned to the helm, he aimed a small handheld flashlight at the instrument panel and the shards of glass at his feet. Peppering the interior of the pilothouse were a few scattered burn marks, once again bringing the mental image of acid spraying all over the boat.

"It doesn't make any sense."

He stepped outside and was blinded by Maggie and the spotlight. Putting a hand over his face, he carefully made his way aft.

"Anything?" Maggie asked.

"No." He groaned, keeping his hand up to shield his eyes. She kept following him with the light, undoubtedly trying to help him see in the dark. "Mind moving that over a bit?"

"Oh." Maggie swung it left. "Sorry."

Julian lowered his arm. "It's alright. Just blinding me for a sec—" His eyes went to the port gunnel where the light had landed. There, he got a good look at the section that had been broken away, forming a near-perfect U-shape in the side.

A single white object stood out. It was wedge-shaped, pointed, had two serrated edges and what appeared to be a calcium base at its bottom.

A shark tooth?

Julian moved to the breach and pried the thing loose. Sure enough, that's what it was.

"Holy shit."

It was two inches long. The tooth itself was white, but there was something off about the base. It had a slimy substance coating it, was greenish-yellow in color, and had a texture like mucus.

"Whoa!" Maggie exclaimed. She moved the light to Willy's fishing rod. Julian looked too, and saw what got her attention.

The line, dangling straight down into the water, was whipping back and forth. It was no different than fishing at the lake back when he was a kid, watching a bluegill trying to run away with his bait before he started cranking them in.

Looking at the line, Julian noticed its tautness. A weight was holding it down at the end.

Probably a shark.

Might as well free it.

Julian moved to the rod, picked it up, and started cranking. Like with lake fishing, he felt resistance. Whatever was on the other end had a decent amount of weight, at least forty to fifty pounds.

It was yanked to one side, then to the other.

"Damn!" Julian fought to control the rod as he brought the thing up. As he did, Maggie centered the light where the line touched the water.

The agent could see some sort of mass below the surface. A flapping caudal fin slapped the water, splashing his face. It was a baby blue shark… *not* hooked to the line, but was actually chewing on some hunk of meat that was.

"What is that?" Maggie asked.

Whatever it was, it wasn't actually hooked, but appeared entangled. The line had wrapped around it many times over. There was an odd, yet familiar shape. Rounded joints, extended limbs…

He raised it out of the water.

…a head, with flesh dissolved, revealing a human skull.

"Jesus!"

Julian released the pole and jumped back, dumping Willy Phelps' severed torso on the deck.

The agent held his breath and fought to keep it together. He stood stiff with his arms out and eyes bulging, taking in the horrible sight. The fisherman had lost everything below the armpits, save for a couple vertebra.

Suddenly, the light moved away. Julian heard a *thump* as Maggie passed out on his flying bridge.

Barely holding it together himself, he made his way over to the boat.

CHAPTER 9

It came as no surprise to Julian that Sheriff Gillis was slow to respond to the call. He and Maggie had waited almost three hours before a pair of police vessels arrived to the scene of the incident.

Maggie remained asleep the whole time. During the wait, Julian gently moved her onto the aft deck and laid out some towels to use as some sort of cushion. Every so often, he checked on her to make sure she was breathing okay. The poor thing was tired, and seeing Willy Phelps' ravaged corpse was the final nail in the coffin.

Her slumber worked in Julian's favor, for it kept her out of sight when the deputies showed up. The last thing he wanted was to be bogged down with unnecessary questions about why he was out on the water alone with Mark Wall's girl. Even in this instance, Julian knew Gillis would devote more attention to that than the death of Mr. Phelps.

The sheriff and the three deputies that showed up with him apparently had things they would rather be doing. One of them was clearly hungover. One of the others kept glancing at his phone. As for Gillis, most of his energy was spent grilling Julian as to why he was out on the water this time of night, as if it wasn't obvious.

Eventually, they got around to towing the boat to the harbor. By the time they arrived, the sun was peeking over the horizon.

A crowd of fishermen had gathered at the pier, awaiting their arrival. It stood to reason that one of the deputies texted somebody about the death of Willy Phelps, and that word quickly spread.

A sick feeling filled his stomach after recognizing Mark Wall's face in the crowd.

Great. Just great.

An EMS unit waited near an ambulance, stretcher set up and ready to go. They began wheeling it down when they saw the sheriff's vessel docking. They zipped the remains in a body bag and loaded it into the ambulance.

Julian moored his boat a couple of spaces down, hoping the crowd's attention would remain fixed on the sheriff. It didn't work.

Like a herd of angry cattle, over two dozen fishermen marched over to his location, barking questions as though Julian himself was somehow responsible.

"The hell's going on? Why's he like that?!" one shouted.

"Why were you out there that late?" another asked.

"Doing my job," Julian replied. "Don't act surprised. Now, listen. There's a bigger issue at play here. I highly recommend everyone stay out of the water until we can determine what happened to Mr. Phelps."

"Oh, you would like that, wouldn't you?" Mark Wall said. "Seeing as you seem dead set on dismantling our honest business."

"That's not it and you know it," Julian replied. He narrowed his gaze at the fisherman. He stood alongside his partner, Glenn, who stared back with a murderous scowl. It was effective enough in getting Julian's heart to thump a little faster. The agent kept his gaze on Mark, doing his best to keep himself calm and collected. "*Somebody's* been dumping toxic waste in your fishing grounds. The feller responsible is costing all of you a lot of money. After all, it's drastically affecting the fish population. Your bounties are either dying off or migrating to healthier waters. What you are bringing in is probably contaminated. I can bring this to a stop if I can find out where the dumping grounds are. I'd hate for you guys to end up eating some fish fillets that may as well be glowing in the dark."

"What does this have to do with Willy?" another fisherman shouted.

Julian looked to where the *Fifth Round* was docked. He could see some of the chemical burns on the hull and structure.

"I can't explain it. On the one hand, he appears to have been attacked by a shark. On the other hand, there are elements that don't add up. It's as though his boat had been sprayed with a corrosive substance."

"Corrosive substance? You mean acid?" someone asked.

"It appears so," Julian said. "I need to run some tests and—"

"Nonsense," Sheriff Gillis called out. He approached from the other dock, thumbs tucked under his duty belt. "Gentlemen, isn't it true that Willy Phelps was talking some nonsense about shark hunting?"

"That's true," Mark Wall said. "He claimed he would go out and hunt for it."

"Illegal shark poaching," Gillis said. His attempt to look as though he gave a damn about the ethics got a head shake from Julian. "I take no pleasure in what happened to Willy, but he went out messing with something he shouldn't have. He paid the price for it. Simple shark attack, that's all it is."

"Sheriff, if I may," Julian said. "The tissue damage, the bite radius—we're talking about a shark of significant size. Maybe twenty-five feet or bigger."

Gillis laughed. "Twenty-five feet. Nonsense! You saw the body, and said yourself that it was in the water getting chewed on by a baby shark.

For all we know, every critter in the ocean took a bite out of him by the time you showed up."

Julian unfortunately couldn't argue against that point, aside from the fact that the spine had been completely severed. Even a full-on feeding frenzy would struggle to do that kind of damage. Nonetheless, he knew bringing it up would be useless. Instead, he went with a different point.

"There's also the issue of the chemical substances on his boat."

"Well, there you go," Sheriff Gillis said. "It stands to reason that Willy Phelps was illegally transporting and dispensing hazardous material into the water. His uncle works for a glass company upstate. There's enough of a connection to put my mind at rest. He went out, did the deed, then decided to illegally poach some sharks. Got himself killed in the process."

A new sick feeling formed in Julian's gut. It was clear that Gillis was trying to shift the blame to Willy Phelps, who was conveniently deceased and unable to refute the claims. It was almost as though he was deliberately trying to bring an end to Julian's investigation by offering a scapegoat.

"Except the traces in the water were not strong enough to suggest Mr. Phelps was dumping in that location," Julian said.

"So what?" Mark said. "He was out in the middle of the night doing something he wasn't supposed to be doing. It stands to reason he's the one tainting the water. Now that he's dead, it won't happen anymore. Shit, I'll bet money he was the one who laid out those drift nets I found yesterday."

"Sounds probable," Gillis added.

Julian couldn't help but chuckle at that. *Well, isn't that convenient?*

He heard a shift in the deck behind him, followed by a groan and an "Ugh! Oh, damn! Where… what happened last night?"

Julian cringed. *Oh, dear God. Maggie, don't sit up. Don't..."*

She sat up.

The crowd of fishermen gasped in unison. Many eyes went to Mark Wall, who watched the pair with burning contempt. Predictably, Sheriff Gillis was quick to turn up the heat.

"So, Mr. Reed, mind explaining why you were out all night with Mark's fiancée?"

"The nerve on this guy," one of the fishermen said. "I guess it's not enough he rode into town and interfered with our livelihoods, but he's now shafting Mark's girl!"

"Nothing of the sort took place," Julian said. He raised his hands defensively as the crowd got increasingly angry. All the while, he studied Mark's expression. The fisherman was angry, but Julian could tell it wasn't for the reason everyone thought was obvious. He was connecting the dots in his head; the agent was out at night with his scorned ex-girlfriend, who probably saw the papers and money he had clumsily left in the garage. It was clear to him what was really going on; she was trying to spoil his new 'career'.

Deep down, Julian was cursing. If only he had those papers, he would have the pleasure of really ruining Mark's day. Better yet, he'd be on his way out of this godforsaken town.

"Why don't you tell them why I'm out here, Mark?" Maggie said.

"Oh, we know," someone shouted from the crowd. "Probably charged him too. Lost her job last night. Probably thought she'd make up the revenue by pursuing other career paths, if you know what I mean."

"Oh, you fuck!" Maggie reached for the deck to climb up and take a swing at the jerk, only for Julian to get in the way.

"Alright, break it up!" Sheriff Gillis said. He faced the crowd. "Everyone, go about your day. Go home, go fishing, get drunk. I don't care. But clear the pier. My men and I need to conduct our investigation of Mr. Phelps' death."

The crowd began to disperse, with a few fishermen tapping Mark Wall on the shoulder to comfort him for Maggie's 'betrayal'. He hardly took notice, for his thoughts were on something a little more dire.

"Come on," he said to Glenn. Together, they walked to the parking lot.

Julian grew nervous as he watched them. The two began a silent conversation as soon as they were out of listening range. It stood to reason they were discussing damage control. After all, they had a loose end.

"Might be a good idea for you to make a call to your supervisor," Sheriff Gillis said.

"Is that right?" Julian said.

"You have your culprit," Gillis said. "No need for you to stick around any longer. I'll write a supplementary report to provide your office. I know this place isn't your cup of tea. Here's your chance to wrap everything up quickly."

Julian crossed his arms. As much as he hated to acknowledge it, even in the depths of his own mind, the thought of a shortcut out of this town was appealing.

His eyes went to Willy Phelps' damaged boat and the strange burns coating the hull. If that wasn't strange enough, there were the impact indentations and bite marks.

The temptation started to dissipate. Something unusual was in the water. Whatever it was, it was related to Mark's operations, whether directly or indirectly. Either way, the curiosity and sense of duty was enough to overpower his desire to leave.

"I can see why you think that's a good idea, Sheriff," he replied.

Gillis gently shifted his stand, squaring up with the agent. He burned him with a murderous glare, silently warning him to heed his advice. Without saying anything further, he stepped away.

Maggie and Julian remained side by side on the pier, the former rubbing her forehead.

"Sorry," she said. "I shouldn't have let them push my buttons so easily."

"Don't worry about it," Julian said.

"And sorry about last night," she added. "I've never seen anything like that in my life."

"No need to apologize for that," Julian said. "I barely kept myself together."

"You think it was a shark?"

He shrugged. It had been a long and exhausting night with no sleep. His mental fortitude was rapidly deteriorating.

"Maybe. I don't know."

She nodded. "So, what do we do now?"

"Now? I'm going to take a snooze," he said. "Then I'm going to write up a report of what happened last night. After that, I'm not sure."

"You're thinking of leaving?" she asked.

Julian didn't answer. He put a hand on her shoulder and walked her to the parking lot.

"Let me drive you back to the hotel. You think you'll be okay?"

Maggie read between the lines. The agent had indeed given up.

"Yeah. I'll be spending all day looking for work," she said.

"Well, if you need a reference for your resume, I'll be happy to help you out," he said.

"Thanks," Maggie said. "I'll need it."

There was no point in arguing the case with Julian. If he had given up, then that was that. It was a world where the bad guys often went unpunished. She may as well keep her head down and accept it.

They got in his truck and began the drive to the hotel.

CHAPTER 10

"Alright baby! Keep it going!"

Brent Doberman and Joey Lemm stuck their tongues out and waved at Julie Garber. The purple and yellow parasail hugged the clear blue sky, its passenger sailing six feet underneath its canopy. The free-spirited Julie Garber held her hands out like wings, letting her male companions below admire the features of her bare torso.

"Oh yeah, baby!" Brent shouted. With one hand on the helm, he looked down at the aft deck of their little cruiser, the *Armadillo*. "Where's Paula?"

Joey smirked. "I think I know."

"Ah." Brent was able to read between the lines. "Tell her not to hog it all. There's four of us."

"I'll say something right now." Joey gripped the ladder, nearly slipping as his obnoxious friend veered suddenly to starboard. Joey squared up with Brent, flexing his abs and biceps in an intimidation display. It only got his fellow high school dropout to laugh.

"Sorry. That doesn't get me wet," Brent said.

Joey continued the scowl, only to eventually break character and join him in laughter. They touched beer bottles and drained their contents, then tossed them into a nearby wastebasket, bringing the count to eight.

"Don't make me fall, man," Joey said.

"Whoops!" Brent shifted the helm to port. This time, Joey had a firm grip on the guardrail. He flipped the bird and descended the ladder. Before entering the cabin, he gave another wave to the flamboyant Julie. She was in her glory, flying twenty-five feet high, naked except for her bikini bottom.

He would probably give thought to having her if he didn't hear the vigorous regimen between her and Brent in his bedroom of their apartment. No huge loss. Paula seemed more interested in him anyway and was just as uninhibited. It was the type the bros generally went for, and Paula and Julie were always available if there wasn't any other tail for them to chase.

Joey entered the cabin and cracked a smile at the sight of Paula bending over the galley table. A two-inch straw separated her nostrils from the white powder coating the small glass board.

He stood there and let her do her thing, admiring the rosebush tattoo on the small of her back.

Paula leaned away from the table and moaned pleasurably, then turned and smiled at the pleasant surprise of Joey's presence.

"Oh! Hey!"

"Enjoying yourself?" he asked.

Paula leaned back against the table, her eyes sharp and ferocious. "Very much so. Not done yet."

Joey liked the sound of that. He put one hand against the doorframe and let his shirt flap open, revealing his muscular frame.

"Yeah? What do you have in mind?" he asked. Paula clicked her tongue and nodded at the window. Joey looked at the greenish-blue waters of the Gulf on the other side of the glass. "What? You wanna parasail?"

"Maybe later. I think I'm up for a swim." Paula didn't wait for a response. She immediately removed her bikini top and bottoms and strutted out the door.

Joey, eager to please his companion, banged his fist on the overhead. "Stop the boat, Brent!"

"Why? Julie's still up there… ohhhh!" As soon as Brent caught sight of Paula, he throttled back and killed the engine.

Paula may have been at a lower altitude, but she was way higher than Julie. She wasted no time diving overboard with a gaudy scream. Joey was right behind her, having ditched his shirt and swim trunks.

They disappeared under the water, reemerging several meters off the port side. Laughing hysterically, they assaulted each other with splashes, which quickly escalated into a robust wrestling match.

Brent remained at the helm, helping himself to another beer while he watched his roommate's escapades. There was no bashfulness regarding lack of decorum. They had shared rooms with two double beds, getting their freak on with whatever dates were willing to spend the night with them.

"Hey! What's going on?!" Julie shouted.

Brent turned his eyes to the sky. She was slowly twirling toward the water, the rounded parasail giving her the appearance of a badminton birdie.

"It's swimming time!" he replied.

"What? No! I wanna keep going! Brent!"

He held his arms out and smirked. "Sorry."

"Brent! I'm gonna kill you! AH!"

She hit the water, the parasail landing on top of her head. It flattened out, her thrashing body forming a bulge in its center.

Joey and Paula started to laugh. They could see the yellow and purple deflated splotch drifting twenty feet away. Its center continued to rise and thrash, with its prisoner howling at them.

"I'm gonna get you assholes for this!"

It only elevated their laughter to even more ridiculous pitches.

After a few moments, Joey and Paula resumed their frolicking. They met in a very vigorous embrace and sank beneath the waves.

Brent's eyebrows twitched. Seeing those two in action was getting him in the mood. He tucked his thumbs under his swim trunks and looked over at Julie.

"Need help over there?"

"YES!"

"On my way, baby." He slipped out of his trunks, made his way to the transom, and prepared to throw himself into the water.

A shriek from Julie brought him to a pause. Brent squinted. That wasn't a playful yell or a shout of frustration. It almost sounded like *terror.*

"OH GOD! BRE—"

The bulge in the parachute rose several feet in the air, then returned to the water. Like a massive fish bobber, it ducked under the water, the parasail cord expanding until it was taut.

"What the hell? Julie?!"

He could see the parachute zigzagging back and forth several yards under the water, its edges enveloping something in its center. The cord tugged and whipped left and right, threatening to snap off its attachment anchor.

As soon as it began, the motion ceased and the canopy rose to the surface.

Brent waited with bated breath, confused and frightened after witnessing the bizarre event. The parasail emerged. It was in tatters, its rounded shape transformed into a hodgepodge of malformed cloth and nylon shreds.

He grabbed the cord and pulled it in.

"Julie?"

The sail, now appearing like a dead jellyfish, followed the line up to the boat. There was some sort of weight under it.

He reached into the water and pulled one side of the sail up, uncovering his fling.

"Jul—"

She was staring up at him, eyes pale and wide, her face bloodless, for it had flushed out through her open stomach. Her breasts were deflated, everything below them having been torn away completely.

Only now did Brent register the faint red cloud dispersing under the water where she had been moments prior. Now, it seemed the blood was rushing from *his* face. He stood there, buck naked, staring at her pasty white corpse.

Panic seized the half-drunk playboy. The world seemed to spin. He felt top heavy, like a tree in a windstorm. Hyperventilation led to dry-heaving, which in turn led to confused babbling.

"Oh, Jesus! Oh, God! Holy… holy…" He sucked in a deep breath, then let out a scream. "H—"

"—OLY FUCK!"

Joey erupted from the ocean like a possessed soul escaping hell, his breath being used to express unparalleled fright. He clawed at the ocean, completely determined to get back to the boat.

Another eruption of water rose from the sea behind him, making way for the author of his fear.

Brent's hyperventilation stopped. It wasn't that he regained control of his composure. Quite the opposite; he was frozen solid as though met with Medusa's stare. All he could do was stand and watch as the great beast lifted its head above the water and drove its teeth into the screaming Paula.

Her head and shoulders stuck out the corner of its mouth, one arm attached to her body only by a few strands of flesh. It dangled like a Christmas ornament, finally falling free after a few shakes.

The beast, with its cigar shape, triangular teeth, and curved fins was unmistakable.

Brent's lip quivered.

"Fucking shark…"

Paula's tongue stuck out of her mouth as the jaws compressed her body. Following a deathly "eeeeeh!" sound, her head fell from the shark's mouth and disappeared into the ocean.

The fish leveled out, angling its head to point one of its green eyes at its next victims.

"Holy Christ!" Finally, Brent managed to snap into action. He moved to the portside guardrail and reached for Joey. "Come on, man! It's coming!"

His effort proved useless.

A swing of its tail propelled the shark to frightening speed like the afterburners to an F-32. The shark did not bother engulfing Joey in its mouth. Instead, it was content with pancaking him between its snout and the hull of the boat.

SLAM!

A wall of water and body parts splashed over the deck.

Brent fell backward, his body finally wetted by the ocean, just not in the way he planned. The boat fishtailed from the impact, adding to his light-headed sense of spinning.

Seated up, he looked at the carnage decorating his deck. An arm lay across from him, a foot a couple of feet to the left, and a string of intestines wrapped around his shoulders like a Hawaiian floral necklace.

"OH MY JESUS!!!"

Brent ripped off the fibrous guts and ran to the ladder. He ascended to the flying bridge and engaged the throttle, forgetting he had switched off the engine a few moments ago.

Cursing with each breath, he fumbled for the key. The engine responded with whirring protests.

All of a sudden, Brent was aware of the tilt in the boat's posture. He turned around and looked into the bloody water where the shark had struck. The port quarter was angling downward, pulled by the weight of seawater that infiltrated through a breach in the hull.

"No, no, NO!"

He twisted the key again, only to get the same pathetic whir.

SPLASH!

Brent looked to starboard. The fish had surfaced, its attention solely on him. It parted its jaws, dangling loose shreds of tissue from the serrated edges of its teeth. Slime dripped from its nostrils and gums, the repugnant smell enough to make the hyperventilating Brent choke for breath.

It appeared to sink back into the water. As it did, it pointed its snout directly at him. In that moment, Brent took notice of the several large pores scattered around its nasal cavities.

Then came the jet of green liquid, and searing pain.

His vision went blank, his eyes burning into his skull. Brent opened his mouth to scream, but could only gargle blood and liquified flesh. Consumed with madness and pain, he clawed at himself to get the burning liquid off, his fingernails scraping his smoking white skull before death finally took hold.

CHAPTER 11

"Sorry. We have no use for you. Best of luck."

All Maggie could do was sport a smile and pick up the tan folder with her resume in it. She knew her luck would be bad, but when even the owner of the crummy Violet Barracuda Bar and Grill was turning her down, she understood the true heights of her misfortune. Working at the counter was an overweight barista with more metal in her face than a plane engine. The clientele were not necessarily people of moderate sensibilities, standards, and ethics. If this place wasn't going to hire her, she really was shit out of luck.

Charlotte Pesko was quick to have her blacklisted. One interesting aspect of the business owners of this town was that there was hardly any sense of competition. In fact, there was a strong sense of community. They often warned each other of surprise inspectors, unruly clientele, and blacklisted employees.

Maggie forced a "thank you" and stepped outside. It was the seventh rejection she experienced today.

Her stomach still ached from the memory of Willy Phelps' mangled corpse being lifted from the water. Her sore back and shoulders from sleeping on the boat added to her discomfort.

She stood in the late afternoon sunlight and watched the world go by. Some of the neon marques lights were switching on. One of them was for the strip joint down the road, Thirteen Podiums. There was always a sign on the door that read *now hiring.*

Maggie felt as if she was an inch tall. She felt like she was staring her future in the face, and it looked miserable. The only thing worse was going hungry and without a roof. By the looks of it, she was going to endure both tonight unless something changed drastically.

Her face tensed and a series of curse words left her lips. After another look at the hunk of junk she drove, she accepted her fate, squared her shoulders, and began marching down the street. Working in the bar, she was constantly getting ogled. Maybe after a few shifts in this joint, she would get used to being naked in front of strangers.

After a few steps, Maggie stopped and looked at the tan folder in her hand. Considering the position she was about to apply for, and the things she heard about the owner, a resume would not be necessary.

She dug her truck keys out of her wallet and turned around. It was at that moment she saw the grey utility van parked a few dozen yards up the street.

It looked eerily familiar, as did the guy in its driver's seat.

Glenn.

Maggie's hands began to tremble. Knowing their partnership, it was probably Mark who greenlit having her tailed. Glenn viewed women as property, and in his mind, Maggie still belonged to Mark. There were only two reasons they would tail her. Either Mark was afraid she would be screwing around, OR they saw her as a loose end that needed to be dealt with.

It was pretty obvious which.

"Shit."

Night would come soon. Glenn was probably waiting for a prime opportunity. He couldn't simply spring at her in broad daylight and snatch her up, not even in this town.

Given her circumstances, he would soon have an opportunity.

Maggie could suddenly relate to small insects she exterminated in the bar and in her house throughout her life. She felt an impending doom, as though she would be stepped on at any given moment.

She weighed her options. Even if she started working tonight in the strip joint, she would end up getting out probably around four. And Glenn would be right there waiting for her.

She needed security. To be around someone who would ensure her safety. The strip joint owner would probably file a police report at some point if she went missing. Maybe.

There was only one place Glenn would not go near. Or rather, a person.

Seeing this as her only hope, she got in her truck and drove to the hotel.

***

Julian Reed sat at the dining table in his hotel room, sipping a beer while he typed away at his computer. He usually hated report writing.

This time, he was flying through it. Considering it was the last one he planned on writing for the EPA.

As he wrote, his eyes repeatedly went to the second window tab on the top of his screen. *Resignation letter.*

He had written it first and planned to send it in at the same time as his report. First, he wanted to cross his T's and dot his I's. Soon enough, he would be back to the quiet, simple life. That was his new ambition. Making a difference in the world? Those were stories for children. All he cared about now was making himself happy.

A knock on the door made him jump. Just a few days in this town naturally made Julian overly cautious. He stood up and slowly walked to the door, hand resting on his sidearm.

"Who is it?"

"It's me. Maggie."

He put his eye to the peephole. Sure enough, it was her. She was quick to enter his room the moment he opened the door.

"Um, come in," he said.

Maggie appeared out of breath as she sat on the edge of the bed. "I'm sorry. I don't mean to bother you again, but um…"

"I take it the job hunt didn't go well," he said.

"No, it didn't," she said. "But that's not why I'm here. I, uh, I think I'm in danger. And you're the only one who might be able to help me." That got Julian's attention.

"What's the matter?"

"I'm pretty sure I'm being followed," Maggie explained. "I was walking a few blocks from here when I saw Glenn's van. You remember what I told you about Glenn, right?"

"Not exactly a saint," Julian replied.

"That's putting it mildly," Maggie said. "Anyway, he's tailing me."

"Have you received any threats or anything like that?" Julian asked. "Any communication at all?"

"None," she said. "Listen, I can't technically prove I'm in danger. Unfortunately, the only way to prove it…"

"Would be to wait and get abducted," Julian finished her sentence.

Maggie sat straight and exhaled, relieved that he understood her plight. Guys who genuinely posed a threat did not always announce their actions. In some cases, they planned in the shadows and made their move at the opportune moment.

"I don't know where else to go. I know you want to get out of this town. I don't blame you for losing faith in your job, and in people in general. What you're going through makes sense. You just see the worst in people, and for every issue you fix, another one takes its place.

There's no real difference being made. At least, that's what you tell yourself. I'm not sure I agree with that, necessarily. But that's beside the point. Please, Julian, is there any way you can help me? I don't know what else to do."

Julian stood silently while he contemplated the issue. He thought of getting Maggie her own room, but realized that would not work. She needed a bodyguard; somebody who was armed.

He absolutely believed her. Maggie was no saint, but she wasn't lying. He knew what fear looked like. Even in the quiet town of Hesperia, there was the odd domestic dispute every once in a while, almost always involving people from out of town. Generally, people stuck in unhealthy relationships. In dealing with those situations, he learned what fear truly looked like, whether it be the eyes of a man, woman, or child.

That same look was plain on Maggie's face.

Julian looked at his room. There was only one bed, which made their situation all the more awkward. He put his hands on his hips and eyeballed the sofa. It wasn't the most comfortable piece of furniture he ever saw, and it definitely was not designed for someone to sleep on, but it looked like he was going to have to make do.

I hate being a gentleman.

"You can have the bed. I'll take the sofa."

Maggie smiled. "Thank you." Right then, she was suddenly aware of the specifications of the room. "Oh! I can take the sofa. It's only fair…"

"No, don't worry about it," Julian said.

Maggie eyed the piece of furniture and lifted an eyebrow. Just looking at it, she knew it wouldn't be comfortable to sleep on. The urge to be polite kicked in.

She moved to one side of the bed and cleared her throat. "There is technically enough room here, if you, uh…" She scratched the back of her head, now hating herself for making this interaction all the more awkward, "…share."

Julian cracked a nervous smile. "I'm… good."

They watched each other in silence, unsure of where to take the conversation from here. Julian rewound his memory to Maggie's plight, which provided an offramp. More importantly, it was an issue that needed to be solved.

"You haven't heard from Mark at all? Or from Glenn?"

"No," Maggie said.

"If they're following you, that might be because they're protecting a significant financial interest," Julian said. "That means, whatever they're dumping into the water, there's even more of it than I thought."

"Like I said, that woman was paying him a lot of money," Maggie said. "For all we know, it was only a down payment. There was a lot of stuff on that list."

Julian looked at the report on his computer screen and sighed. He was so close to being done with this place. He could feel the angel and devil on his shoulders, whispering in his ears, one telling him to say 'to hell with this' and finalize the report, the other appealing to his better nature. Maybe if Maggie wasn't here, the uglier side would have won.

However, something about her presence inspired something good in him.

His gaze met hers. She was no longer afraid. On the contrary, she was thankful.

"You up for another boat ride?" he asked.

Maggie smiled. "I think I am." That smile vanished after another concern put itself front and center in her mind. "But, what about Willy Phelps? The shark, or whatever it was that killed him. What if we run into that? You were saying something wasn't normal about it."

"There were chemical burns on that boat," Julian said. "I can't confirm what caused them. And I won't be able to unless I find whatever your ex-boyfriend is dumping in the ocean."

"Okay. Let's do it, then." Maggie stood up and walked with him to the door. "This might be a dumb question, but how could pollutants affect the sea life? I mean, would it just kill them? Or would it do something else? Like affect their DNA?"

"Depends on the species, the type of contaminants, and the level of exposure," Julian said. "Yeah, in most cases, it would result in death. In other cases, it could result in something else."

"Like what?"

"Mutation."

CHAPTER 12

"Nothing here." Julian hoisted the underwater drone back onto the deck of the boat. It was one-thirty in the morning, and the needle-in-a-haystack routine was getting really tiresome. There was a reason those slimebags were dumping their shit in the ocean. As long as there were no witnesses, the stuff would be near-impossible for anyone to find.

Maggie approached him with a large thermos. "Need some more fuel?"

Julian picked up his coffee mug and extended it in her direction. "Don't mind if I do."

As soon as the black liquid heaven reached the brim, he started sucking it down. Maggie took great pleasure in watching him enjoy it.

"That ought to do the trick."

"That it should," Julian replied. He took one more chug, concluding with a satisfied "Ah!" He carried the mug to the bridge and put a hand on the helm, watching the sea while trying to figure out where to go next. "Any other ideas?"

Maggie looked at their surroundings, admiring the beautiful, but haunting blackness of the sea. "These are his fishing grounds. A few years ago, while griping to his buddies during a slow season, he complained of poor catch at the Whitecap Ridge."

Julian looked the location up on a map of the area he had downloaded. Interestingly, it was a deeper location with a sizable gorge in the seabed.

"Holy crap! Why didn't you mention it before?"

"Because I forgot the place even exists. I only remember the name of that place, because in that same conversation, Mark decided to brag to his friends about—" Her voice trailed off. "Nevermind."

A few minutes went by before Julian realized he was staring. He was able to read between the lines. Evidently, Mark had a few fetishes and Maggie was the object of his pleasure. It was one thing when two people genuinely loved and felt attraction for one another, but their relationship sounded more and more like she was treated as an object to be used rather than a human being.

"I get the idea." He throttled the boat northwest. For the next few minutes, he enjoyed the rest of his coffee while feeling the salty breeze in his hair. "He's a fool, you know?"

Maggie perked up. "Mark?"

Julian held up his mug. "Anyone who can make a cup of coffee this good deserves a lot better, if you ask me."

He cringed at his own statement. It was meant to sound funny and fill in the boring silence, but came off as if he was hitting on her. The fact he was aware she was recently single did not help that appearance.

Maggie cracked a smile. "I am a bartender. We serve more than whiskey." She moved up to the helm and stood beside him. Julian felt simultaneously excited and uncomfortable by her presence.

You're on the job. Besides, she's not your type.

"Or, you've only ever had cheap Keurig single-serve coffee," she added. "Compared to that stuff, anything tastes like a five-star product."

Julian grinned. "Is it *that* obvious?"

"Considering your praise for my coffee, I'd say so. But I appreciate the compliments all the same."

"I'm cheap," he said. "I'm always on the go, and I don't make as much as people think. Then again, I'm a simple guy. I like steak and mashed potatoes, scrambled eggs and bacon… pie. Mm-mmm."

"No shame in that," Maggie said. "I guess it explains why you want to go back to that little town you're from. Simple guy wanting to live the simple life."

"You've got me pegged," he said. "I like trees, lake water, mild winters."

"And not people?"

"Ha." Julian thought of the best way to respond to that. "I like people well enough. Certain ones. I just don't like crowds." He looked over at her. "I suppose that sounds silly to you, considering the setting you've lived in all your life."

"Are you kidding?" she exclaimed. "That sounds great. I've been trapped here. Haven't been able to afford a car that can go a year without having ten-thousand dollars' worth of repairs needed. Half my customers don't tip. My credit is in the toilet. My job opportunities are, let's just say, not great. Not to mention the majority of the population is not known for their good character. So, no, what you described sounds like heaven."

Julian was intrigued. Admittedly, he did not think of Maggie as one with a complex mind. But the more time he spent with her, he truly felt how the walls were closing in around her. She was at rock bottom in a place she absolutely did not want to be.

"What would you do?" he asked. "I mean; if you could snap your fingers and make a change, what would you do? Where would you live? How would you make a living?"

"In Vegas, winning blackjack, drinking mojitos!" she joked.

Julian snorted, his new view of her threatening to revert to his original judgements.

Maggie finished laughing at her joke, then gave the question some serious thought. She was staring into the distance, occasionally opening her mouth to speak, but stopping herself. It was the action of someone who felt embarrassed about her answer.

"Anything you say is safe with me," he quipped.

She smiled nervously. "If you insist… I've fantasized about opening my own diner."

"Oh?"

"Nothing fancy. Fifteen tables and a bar, serving breakfast, lunch, and dinner."

"I didn't realize you enjoyed cooking so much."

"Shit, I *love* cooking!"

Julian was pleasantly assured by her burst of enthusiasm. It brought out a vibrant energy in her that he found endearing. The tattooed, biker girl exterior was a product of her environment. In a sense, she had no choice. Out here, one needed to have a razor's edge in their attitude. But beneath all that was a woman with aspirations.

"Anything's possible."

Maggie's upbeat attitude quickly deflated. "I appreciate your naïve viewpoint. But I'm screwed."

"No, you're not. So, you're in a rough spot, but I think anything's possible. You'll pull yourself out of it."

Maggie shook her head. "How cute. You're one of those 'pull yourself up by the bootstraps' type of guys."

"Okay, answer me this," he said. "Have you ever heard a success story about someone who *didn't* have to pull themselves up by the bootstraps? Honestly. Think about it."

Maggie moved away from the helm. Julian, seeing her mood freefall, questioned whether he said the right thing. Sure, it was a hard truth, but maybe now was not the time for her to hear it.

On the other hand, such things were usually painful to hear when one was in her position. When the weight of the world was crushing someone, the whole idea of pulling themselves out of it did not feel plausible.

She remained quiet for a little longer, leading Julian to suspect she was giving his point some consideration.

Then she spoke.

"Easy for you to say. You're the one who has the luxury of *leaving* his career. 'Oh, wahhh, I'm not making a difference, so I wanna retreat to the town that time forgot.' Yeah, you're not rich, but you aren't boxed in. Me? I have to catch whatever falls through the cracks. Sure, I could've made better choices in the past, but I didn't know better. It doesn't change that I'm at a point *now* where I have almost no way out. Christ, I'd be lucky to get a job as a stripper."

She noticed the look on Julian's face.

"Yeah, I was gonna go for an interview before I noticed I was being tailed. Put yourself in my shoes and tell me how you'd do anything different."

The shift in the conversation caught Julian off guard. He was no stranger to getting on people's bad side, but in almost every circumstance, it was an instance where he would never see them again. But with Maggie, he was stuck with her the rest of the night.

Damn, we're not even together, and I'm still in the doghouse.

"I guess… I would…" He stammered, worried that whatever he would say next may be interpreted as insulting.

THUMP!

He fell against the helm. "What the hell?"

Maggie stumbled as well.

In the blink of an eye, the topic was forgotten.

Julian slowed the boat to a stop and leaned over the side to look at the hull. "What the hell did I hit?"

Maggie looked over the starboard side. "I'm not sure. I see some scrapings. It almost looks like… wait… I saw something."

Julian moved to her side, catching a glimpse of a splash thirty feet out.

"Oh, God. I hope we didn't hit a dolphin or something."

"It'd be the world's dumbest dolphin," Maggie said. "I know this much: they're not usually in the habit of getting in front of boats."

Another break in the water caught their eye. This time, it was directly in front of the bow, moving left.

Julian aimed his light, illuminating a dorsal fin and the top lobe of a dark caudal fin six feet behind it.

"That's no dolphin."

The fish hooked in their direction. By now, its entire back was exposed in the glow of the spotlight.

"Wait a minute… what's wrong with it?" Maggie said.

Julian stared, puzzled, at the green secretion coming from the animal's gill slits. It drifted on the water's surface like oil. A terrible odor permeated the air, concluding that this stuff was not a figment of their imaginations.

It lifted its head, revealing blood-red eyes, green wedge-shaped teeth, and veiny blue flesh. Those mighty jaws parted and made contact with the vessel.

Thump!

The creature thrashed, attempting futilely to bite a chunk out of the hull.

Julian clung to the guardrail, unsure if he was fascinated or utterly terrified by what he was witnessing. This was far beyond typical behavior for a shark of any species. Contrary to what was depicted in fiction, sharks generally preferred to go for weak or injured prey, or better yet, food that was already dead. Attacking boats many times their size was way beyond normal.

To say something was wrong with this fish was the understatement of the century. In addition to its behavior was its bizarre appearance. The creature actually appeared to be secreting some sort of substance. The strange odor did not resemble anything biological. It didn't smell like diseased tissue, ejected stomach contents, or waste. If anything, it almost resembled industrial odors, possibly from some sort of chemical plant.

The creature lacked the bite power to damage the hull beyond a few tiny grooves. It lashed its tail back and forth, doing its best to 'kill' the boat. There was no fear, nor was there any regard for the fact it was not gaining sustenance.

All he could do was mutter, "What in God's name?"

Maggie squinted. "Hold on a sec…" She reached over and grabbed one of Julian's spare flashlights.

"What's the matter?"

"I thought I saw smoke."

Julian's first instinct was to chuckle. Had it not been for the fact this was already supremely unusual, he would have.

She beamed the light at the area where the shark was biting. "Julian? There *is* smoke!"

He leaned farther down. "You sure it's not just mist or…" He stopped mid-sentence, seeing the thin plume of gas that definitely was not mist. Its color appeared greyish in the light and it billowed directly from a strange green substance that spewed from some pores in the shark's snout.

Watching intently, he observed the marks in the hull. Slowly, but truly, that substance was eating its way into the boat.

"Holy shit!"

"What is it?" Maggie said. "Acid?"

"I don't know, but that shark's not gonna leave us alone." He parted from the forward gunnel and found his service pistol.

Shooting a wild animal was definitely *not* what he had in mind when he joined the EPA. The thought made him sick. At the same time, he wasn't willing to sink to the bottom of the Gulf for his conscience.

He returned to the gunnel and took aim at the shark. "Cover your ears, Maggie."

She quickly did so.

Julian squeezed off several rounds. A group of six holes popped open across the shark's head. It corkscrewed in place, jetting dark blood from its wounds. More of that strange fluid spewed from its gills and the back of its throat.

Julian leaned back and pinched his nose. "Holy Mother of—"

Maggie was doing the same. Her face appeared nearly as green as the stuff in the water.

"Geez! What is wrong with that thing?"

Julian watched as the shark's motions slowed. The tail ceased its slashing motions and the jaw went slack. The fish, now literally dead weight, sank under the swampy waves.

"For starters, it's dead," he replied.

"If you ask me, you did it a favor," Maggie said. "That thing was sick as hell." She froze in a moment of reflection. "Didn't you say something about a mutation from toxic exposure?"

"That I did," Julian said. "And that's probably what happened to it." He went to the aft deck in search of his drone. He dug out a tether and a hook to attach to its end.

"What do you have in mind?" Maggie asked.

"I'm gonna use my drone to get a line on the shark so I can haul it up. We're gonna tow it back to shore. Get me my phone, will ya? I know a guy who can help me examine this thing. And whatever you do, don't touch that slime stuff."

Maggie was already moving away from the gunnel, hands raised in disgust. "You don't have to tell me twice. You think that shark is what caused the damage to Willy Phelps' boat? There were chemical burns there, too."

Julian started to sweat.

"Whatever he encountered was much bigger." He looked into the water, dreading what secrets were lurking underneath its surface.

His stomach tightened.

The drone dropped into the water. Julian sped the thing to the seafloor as fast as he could in search of the dead shark, all the while, keeping an eye on their surroundings.

Never in his life did he want to get on land so badly.

CHAPTER 13

"Uh-huh… yeah, I understand… So, what if Wall is heading out there tomorrow? Why does it matter if I'm getting this done early? I just want it over with… Yeah, I'm well aware the treehugger is snooping around. What does it matter?... The odds that he'll find that place are slim to none… No freaking way, I'm not going to a different spot. There's a reason I head out there. Nobody fishes that area anymore. It's deep enough that nobody notices anything out of the ordinary… Thank you. I'll meet you tomorrow."

Isaac Crogen ended his call and turned to face his first mate. "Sweet Jesus, that woman."

His mate, a dark-skinned man of six-foot-five by the name of Halbrook Jennings, fastened a bungee cord around the eight barrels huddled on their aft deck.

"She micromanaging again?"

Isaac removed his burnt-down cigarette and used its orange tip to light a fresh one. "She's growing paranoid because that agent is still in town. Apparently, Mark's girl has been seeing him. *Ex-girl*, I should emphasize. I guess she moved out."

Halbrook chuckled. "Uh-oh! And she's trying to get even by spilling the beans."

"Mark claims she doesn't know anything. The chick is… was… a bartender. The only time she's been offshore has been to sunbathe on the deck of his boat. She has no idea where anything is. And she has no way of finding out, either."

"What does the client want?" Halbrook asked. He was glancing at the lot overlooking the pier where their vessel, *Bluefin*, was moored. It was a small public area a couple of miles south of the harbor; the best available location for them to fulfill their contract with Ria Thorne. A signed piece of paper in this regard only guaranteed them their pay. In a sense, it allowed both parties to blackmail the other should one not hold up their end. However, it did not shield the fishermen from legal ramifications of what they were setting out to do.

"She wants us to choose a new location to dispose of the shit," Isaac said.

"What's the problem with that?" Halbrook asked.

"The farther out we spread this shit, the more likely it is someone will find it," Isaac replied. "Sure, it's a needle in a haystack, but the EPA has someone looking for that needle. If we spread the stuff out, we kill a wider stretch of the ecosystem." There was no compassion in his voice, only a plain matter-of-fact tone. "Obviously, the agency felt enough of a concern to send the country boy out here. So far, he has found nothing, as far as I know. But if we spread the stuff out and fuel their probable cause, more agents might show up."

Halbrook nodded. Isaac's concern was simple. The more agents there were, the greater the likelihood they would find the barrels. Such a result was bad for both the company and those they were paying under the table to dispose of their waste.

He untied the mooring lines, separating the boat from the pier.

Isaac throttled out and headed northwest.

It was his fifth shipment made in the service of Ms. Thorne. He still did not know the name of her company, nor did he care. As long as the cash was handed over, he was content in their secrecy.

He counted all of his cash before coming out to his boat. The payment was enough to pay off his crappy, mold-infested house and his rusty shrimp boat, and leave plenty extra for him to feel rich. In the back of his mind, he knew those pleasures would be short-lived. Halbrook was a guy who loved spending money on trivial things, and the more he had, the more he spent. A more responsible man would use his funds to repair his house or scrap it and put a down payment on a newer, healthier one. But Halbrook was too cheap for that. Just the fact he was considering paying the place off entirely was his best demonstration of financial discipline in all of his existence.

Isaac was not much different. His housing situation was better than his captain's, though only marginally. He lived in an apartment, which he only used for sleeping and having his way with any woman who would give him the time of day. Otherwise, his personal time was spent at the bar or the casino.

Halbrook knew the guy had already lost most of his cut in blackjack. This recent payment would be the first mate's last chance to keep his head above poverty for a while. The fishing had been hell recently, largely thanks to their new side hustle. Even the last few seasons prior to this had been lackluster. Halbrook was told his low quantities were because he fished the same areas over and over and over again, and never adjusted his strategies. But he, being the type who knew best, often responded with, "No, man. They're just dying out."

If it wasn't true then, it was now.

Halbrook didn't care. His financials were taken care of.

He brought the boat three quarters of a mile from shore, watching the black ocean glimmer in the reach of his forward spotlight. Isaac prepared the pulley system connected to the portside outrigger and hooked up one of the barrels. They were still a few miles from their destination, but it was good to be ready to go once they got there. Halbrook wanted the job done quickly so he could return and receive the second half of their payment.

"Hey Cap?"

"What is it?" Halbrook said, keeping his eyes forward while listening to some golden oldie tunes on his radio.

"There's something in the water," Isaac said.

Halbrook switched the radio off and turned to look. Isaac was beaming one of the spotlights into the water. In its glow was a rectangular object with crooked edges. It was wooden in appearance, having been broken at both ends.

A wooden railing.

Interesting, but hardly anything worth his attention. Halbrook opened his mouth with intent to say exactly that.

Then he noticed something else emerge in the white glow—a red inflatable donut with ten feet of rope attached to it.

Beyond the inflatable was another piece of wreckage drifting in the water.

Then another.

And another.

By now, Halbrook knew that was the appropriate word. *Wreckage.*

He moved to the port side of the flying bridge and laid eyes on at least fifteen pieces of decking and fishing gear.

"Holy shit, what the hell happened?"

Isaac tilted his nose up, his shock turning into disgust as he sniffed. "What's that smell?"

Halbrook noticed it too.

"Fuel, maybe?"

Isaac shook his head. "I've worked around fuel long enough to know it doesn't smell like that. Not even while burning. No, this is something else."

Taking another whiff of the whatever-it-was in the air, Halbrook nodded in agreement.

The more important question was 'whose boat is this?' Furthermore, there was the issue of 'What the hell do I do?'

He couldn't make a call to the Coast Guard—especially not with the cargo currently aboard his vessel. Radioing the sheriff would probably result in some people from the state coming out here too. On the other hand, he couldn't just not report the situation either.

Halbrook was a self-centered human being, no question. He wore it on his sleeve. But he was not completely inhuman.

"Let's see if there are any survivors," he said.

Isaac glanced at their cargo. "Um…"

"The only person from Pelican Grove who fishes out here this late, that I know of, is Gerry Grey." He turned the boat to port and slowly advanced west. "Of course, it could be someone from up the panhandle, or…"

More wreckage drifted into view. Pieces of netting, bait, and miscellaneous material expanded in all directions from a singular epicenter. In-between them all was a strange, slimy material. In Halbrook's mind, he thought of the stuff as snot. It was wet and had a way of clinging to whatever it touched.

Some of it made contact with the hull of the *Bluefin*, instantly clinging to it like a spider's webbing.

Isaac beamed his light directly at the goop. It was dark green in color and radiated with a terrible smell.

In addition to that, the two men detected another, more distinct odor. This one irritated the back of their throats. Halbrook waved his hand in front of his nose as if that would do any good. He thought back to a cookout he attended. The guy on the grill acted as if he was some five-star chef, but in reality, he had no damn clue what he was doing. He added a mixture of spices to some chicken breasts that were already overcooked. Too many spices and too much of each one resulted in an odor that was literally *painful.*

Compared to whatever was in the air now, that dumbass' recipe was heaven.

Isaac was clearing his throat. "What *is* that?"

Halbrook noticed the air in the spotlight. They were moving through smoke.

He shifted the spotlight up ahead.

"Holy..."

He stopped the boat and stepped away from the helm. Isaac leaned over to get a look at whatever was in front of them.

At first glance, they thought they were looking at a waterspout. A transparent, twisting form reached all the way to the clouds.

Smoke.

At its base was the bow of an eighty-foot trawler. Its hull was black, with many parts of it spewing the toxic gas. The outriggers were busted and much of the hull had numerous breaches. There was no cratering around the edges of each breach that would indicate some sort of impact. The metal around them was highly discolored and thinned.

Chemical burns.

Isaac had a hand on his stomach. "Cap?"

"I know," Halbrook muttered. His first mate wanted to turn back. Halbrook was giving it some thought. He had seen the aftermath of Willy Phelps' boat. It too, had suffered significant chemical burns that had nearly sunk the thing.

What alarmed him more was the state of the fisherman himself. He heard Phelps had been bitten in half. Prior to that, he had gotten entangled in his own fishing line.

Halbrook had fished once with him. Just on that one trip alone, Phelps had accidentally walked into his own outstretched line, and after getting flustered, he had twisted around and gotten himself tied up.

In addition, he remembered hearing his story of a huge shark that ran away with his catch. Halbrook, like everyone else, laughed the guy out of the bar. Even after his death, nobody thought anything of it.

Now? Halbrook felt like the crazy one.

He turned the wheel to port.

"We heading back?" an eager Isaac asked.

"Damn right we are. We'll get our stuff in the trailer, then we'll give Gillis a call. Then we'll—"

A sound of splashing water made Halbrook bounce on his toes. Somewhere behind the *Bluefin* came a sound almost identical to a whale spouting.

Both men turned their eyes to the transom. The ocean behind their boat was churning, having been disturbed by some large mass.

Rising from the water was thick smoke—the same kind that was rising from the wreckage.

Halbrook had no intention of staying around and trying to figure out what was in the water. He engaged the throttle and sped the *Bluefin* eastwards.

Clank! Clank! Clank! Clank! Clank!

His heart skipped a beat.

"Oh, no, no, no!" he stammered. This was the absolute worst time to be suffering some sort of mechanical failure.

The sound was coming from aft, below the waterline.

In the next few moments, the *Bluefin* lost all speed.

He tried throttling back. He heard the whirring of the prop, but got no motion.

Isaac hurried to the transom with a flashlight in hand. Folding himself over the coaming, he aimed the light into the water to get a few of the propellers.

"You see something?"

Isaac leaned back. His face was red while he coughed his lungs out. By that point, Halbrook could see the smoke rising from behind the transom.

Isaac turned to face him. "I think the propellers…" His voice trailed off and he broke eye contact, as if feeling foolish about his report.

"Well, what?" Halbrook said.

"I think they're *gone*," Isaac said.

Halbrook stood dumbfounded. "They're what?"

"Gone! Like, the blades are no longer there." Isaac took another glance over the back of the vessel. "There's all sorts of burn marks back here. It's almost like…" He paused, his spotlight aimed outward at something else that obviously had his attention.

SPLASH!

CRUNCH!

A wall of water erupted from behind the transom.

Isaac's lower half fell backwards, spilling intestines over the broken segment of spinal column onto the deck. Everything above the bellybutton was gone.

Halbrook shuddered.

A torpedo-shaped form coursed through the water's surface, trailing bits of meat from Isaac's upper half. A half-moon-shaped tailfin swung left and right, propelling the huge fish through the water. A huge dorsal fin cleaved the air, slowly hooking to the right.

Just as Willy Phelps had said, it was a *shark*.

A huge, pissed-off, fucked up shark!

From its gill slits came large globs of that weird slimy stuff. Its snout appeared rigid and oddly crooked, with one particularly large pore behind the nostrils.

It came at the *Bluefin* at high speed.

BAM!

Halbrook clung to the helm as the boat teetered to starboard. The shark pressed the assault, biting at the hull, marking the fiberglass with its teeth.

The captain was lost in a whirlwind of terror. He started twisting the ignition key, forgetting that the boat was already running.

He shifted into full-throttle.

The engine roared, yet it did not move forward.

Raising its caudal fin, the shark turned around and smacked the side of the *Bluefin*, sending it into a slow tailspin.

Halbrook realized there was no escape. He moved down the ladder and made his way to the galley, where he kept his double-barrel shotgun. Two twelve-gauge shells were loaded and ready to go.

He returned topside and moved to the portside gunwale. Shouldering the weapon, he watched the distortions in the ocean from the shark's wake. It was moving towards him to attempt another bite of his vessel.

Jittery fingers squeezed the trigger prematurely, delivering a volley of pellets at the oncoming predator.

Some of those struck its snout. Though no damage was visible, Halbrook assumed he must have hurt the fish, as it quickly jerked to its right and swam off.

It only retreated a dozen yards or so before circling back.

Halbrook breached the shotgun and loaded two fresh shells. Inhaling deeply, he regained control over himself.

Just wait for it to get closer. Let it get within one or two yards of the hull, then blow a huge hole in its head.

The creature was moving in, its ugly face high above the water, sporting that devilish grin.

Halbrook moved to the transom for a better shot, pausing momentarily after stepping in the pool of Isaac's insides.

He summoned the courage and took position, weapon at eye level, pointed downward at the oncoming fish.

"I see you, you ugly son of a bitch," he muttered. "Come on. Do your worst."

The shark closed within two yards.

Suddenly, a thick stream of green fluid spewed from that pore in its snout.

Halbrook's vision disappeared.

In the blink of an eye, he was in a world of burning pain.

Halbrook dropped his shotgun and clawed at his face. "Agh! AAGGHH!!!"

His skin peeled under his bony fingertips. Their tips came over the hollow slots that were his eye sockets, which now served as pools for red goo. His cheeks dissolved and dripped down his chest, revealing his poor dental work.

Halbrook collapsed, his back striking one of the sizzling hot barrels of waste. The acid burnt through the metal shell and made contact with the contents inside.

BOOM!

The huge vibrations and bright orange flash traveled far and wide, overwhelming the shark's senses. There was no more food to be taken from the large, floating object that carried the humans.

It moved eastward to distance itself from the warm waters and the chemical mixtures that burned on its surface. Hunger and self-preservation were the only two factors that guided its actions, and the former was driving its mind to the brink of insanity.

To satisfy its urge, the fish scanned the water for any signs of new prey. It was not until it had swum two hundred yards east of the wreckage that it picked up new vibrations. The source was far away; maybe a little more than a half mile, and in shallow water.

The fish quickened its pace. Nerves all across its body fired pain signals to its brain. It was a constant hell, one the fish thought was normal. It was a hell that put it on the offensive twenty-four-seven, as those in the shallow water were about to find out in brutal fashion.

CHAPTER 14

Joe Lewey splashed in the moonlight, happily pursuing his two companions into deeper water.

The evening had been a fruitful one. He had gone downtown for some entertainment, getting quite a bit while shoving dollar bills into the panties of very attractive dancers. He had become a regular customer for them and, considering how much money he slipped their way, they enjoyed the process. Joe Lewey was average-looking at best for someone in his mid-thirties. He was not obese, but did not have the most attractive build. But he paid quite a bit of green paper for the things he wanted, almost giving off the false impression that he was wealthier than he actually was.

Tonight's striptease proved most entertaining for the pizza delivery driver. The two ladies at his booth, Kayla and Marie, struck up small talk with him while they did their work.

During that time, one of them let it slip how they were behind on rent. They lived in the same apartment and, like many people in this town, blew their finances on things they didn't need, leading to them falling behind on actual necessities like rent and groceries.

Joe Lewey was a man who had an eye for opportunity. He never used it for anything constructive, such as building his career or improving his physical health. It was always for more self-centered, entertaining prospects.

"What if I said I could give you ladies five hundred bucks?"

It was a question that immediately gained a lot of enthusiasm from his two entertainers.

"If you said that, then I'd say, 'oh, my, Mr. Lewey, however can we repay you?'" Marie had replied.

It was precisely what he had hoped to hear. He had both women in the palm of his hand. From the looks of it, they were extremely open to suggestion. Though nobody would dare acknowledge it, the two strippers were gladly willing to whore themselves to him in exchange for cash.

And Joe could not be happier.

Of course, his first thought was to take them to his apartment. But, somehow, that seemed *too* simple. If he was buying himself a night with these ladies, he wanted to add some extra kick to the experience. It was summer time in Florida. What better way to enjoy some two-in-the-morning adventure than a swim.

Kayla was several feet ahead of him, backstroking alongside Marie. They were holding hands, their feet moving up and down like dolphin flukes. Graceful movements kept them afloat and beyond the reach of their eager 'companion'. It was a tease that spurred Joe on.

"You look like you're struggling there, Joe," Kayla said.

He slowed down and tried to catch his breath. They were in eight feet of water now. It was in moments like this where Joe remembered swimming was not exactly his strong suit. It was one thing to frolic in the shallows, but actual swimming, where he had to actually apply effort to keeping his head above the water, was more work than he imagined—even while skinny dipping with two smoking hot strippers.

"No, I'm good!" he lied.

He kept going after them.

The women continued moving with graceful, natural movements, and what appeared to be a superhuman ability to effortlessly remain afloat.

The whole idea was for him to chase them out into deeper water. There was a thrill to the thought of catching them and escalating into a three-way makeout session. Then again, in that fantasy, he never felt fatigue, and had borderline superhuman strength.

In real life, the thrill was short-lived.

Should've just taken them to the stupid apartment.

That thought, which originally seemed too plain, was more appealing than ever.

Joe slowed to a stop.

"What's the matter, big guy?" Marie called out with a laugh.

Joe, smiling to save face, began backstroking to shore. "You win, girls. I need to head back before I drown."

Kayla burst out laughing. "Already? We've only been out here for a few minutes, and you're already calling it quits?"

Joe tried to take that statement as nothing more than a playful jab.

Making an unenthused chuckle, he responded, "I just need my feet to touch the bottom. Everything becomes a little too much work after that."

"Aw!" Marie waved at him as though to say farewell.

Joe moved closer to shore, swinging his feet over the sea bottom in hopes of standing upright. He still had a little farther to go.

Meanwhile, the girls began splashing each other, screaming with joy.

Joe was all at once amused and bothered. He liked seeing them in such a good mood. After all, living out his fantasy would be difficult if the ladies were not so happy. On the other hand, their joy was coming more from one another than him.

Subconsciously, he got nervous.

Are they under the impression they would only screw me if I managed to catch them?

It was a theory that seemed a little too plausible.

To test it, he waved to Kayla and Marie. "Come join me over here!" They continued their little game, not even acknowledging his invite. Joey waited a few more moments, then called to them again.

"Come over here with me!"

This time, Kayla looked over at him. "Nah! You come out *here!*"

"You want something, you'll have to work for it, Joey boy!" Marie called out.

Joey's sense of excitement wafted away. He was feeling something he would not in a million years think he would experience while spending the night with two strippers: frustration.

"No, *you* come over *here*!" he replied.

It came out a little more aggressive than he intended.

"Um, you set the rules, Joe," Kayla said. Her tone was a little less playful than it had been.

"Yeah, and I'm the one paying your rent," he replied.

The two strippers stared at him.

In the blink of an eye, the mood was gone.

"When we came out here, we asked what you had in mind," Marie called out.

"Yeah, and you then said 'go out as far as you can. I'll give you a head start. If I catch you, you know what that means,'" Kayla added. "You didn't catch us. Obviously, you know what that means."

Joe's eyes bulged.

"It means I'm ready for you to join me over here."

"For what?" Kayla said.

He tried to give her the benefit of the doubt. That *had* to be a sarcastic response. He had given them five hundred dollars for crying out loud. Did they think they could just get out of it with some loophole in his logic. He still planned on taking them to his place after they dried off. He just thought some water action would be a nice appetizer to the main course.

"Very funny," he said. "Come on. In the words of *Scorpion*, 'Get over here!'"

Kayla waved her finger. "Ah-ah-ah! You made the rules."

Shedding all remainder of his good-will, Joe hammered the water with his fists.

"Listen, bitches. *I'm* paying *you*! The rules are what I say they are."

The two women looked at him, astonished. They were caught between their own egos and the reality of their situation. It was true that the date for paying rent was nigh, and they were short on cash. On the other hand, as free-spirited as they were, it was hard to subject themselves to the desires of someone who openly spoke to them in this manner.

"Geez!" Marie exclaimed. "Had I known you'd be like this, I wouldn't have bothered coming out here with you."

"No shit!" Kayla said.

Joey backed up a few steps and crossed his arms. "So, that's it? You're suddenly not up for the task?"

They looked at each other, then at him.

"Go fuck yourself," Kayla said.

"Literally," Marie added with a laugh.

Joe sneered. "Alright, fine. You can stay here for all I care. Enjoy getting evicted."

Kayla held up a middle finger.

Joe returned the gesture. "Oh, and good luck finding a ride."

"I doubt we'll have a problem," Marie called back.

Joe waved her off. "You know what? Stay out in the water. Get eaten by a shark while you're at it."

The women cackled at him in an obnoxious manner designed to trigger a reaction.

Joe threw a few curse words in their direction, then turned around and marched to shore.

The laughter was constant, right up until a colossal *SPLASH!*

In a heartbeat, that laughter transformed to screaming.

Joe turned around, seeing Kayla being lifted several feet out of the water. He could only see her head, shoulders, and arms. Everything else had vanished into the mouth of a huge SHARK!

The beast stuck straight up out of the water as though balancing on its tail. It maintained that pose for half-a-second, then splashed down. On its way, those jaws closed the rest of the way.

Kayla's upper body *popped* from its mouth like a cork from a champagne bottle, trailing guts while skipping across the water's surface.

Its massive tail arched skyward before slamming into the ocean, mere feet from where Marie was.

She was making her way to shore. No longer was her swimming graceful and sensuous, but clumsy and chaotic. Bent fingers clawed the water, pulling her ever-closer to safety.

Joe moved deeper until only his tiptoes could touch the bottom. He reached out to Marie.

"Come on! Come on!" he said.

She saw the gesture and came his way.

A mountain of water rolled in her direction. It split apart, revealing the demonic face of the predator. Its jaws were clamped shut, its eyes rolling back.

Another wave encompassed Marie.

She threw her arms upward and began screaming at the top of her lungs. The spray of fluid splattered over her shoulders and rained down over Joe's outstretched arm.

Immediately, he felt a magnitude of heat and pain he did not think was possible. One time, he had accidentally touched a frying pan that had literally just come off the stove. That alone left an impression that Joey never forgot.

Compared to this, Joe would gladly *lick* off that sizzling pan.

Before his very eyes, his hand dissolved. He watched in agony and disbelief, seeing his five digits drip into the ocean, their bones briefly visible before they, too, disintegrated.

In a matter of seconds, there was nothing below the wrist.

A few feet ahead of him, Marie's entire upper body was undergoing the same process. Her hair and facial features were gone, leaving skeletal hands clutching a screaming skull.

Behind that living corpse was the shark.

Joe turned around. With large strides, he made his way to shore, not daring to look back. The water fell to his bare waist, then to his ankles. His lackluster swimming skills and loss of a hand did not hinder the speed of his retreat. He successfully arrived onto the beach, with only forty feet to go before reaching his vehicle.

It could've been a thousand feet away for all he cared. He was on land now.

Okay, you're ashore—safe from the shark...

He heard the splashing of water hitting his back preceding the entry of thirty teeth entering his flesh.

The shark rolled on the beach like a log, munching its prey while nudging itself back to the sanctuary of its natural habitat. Spewing secretions from its gills and leaving behind severed limbs, it managed to scoot westward. It put its caudal fin to work, slithering like a worm off of the sandbar.

A minute later, it was swimming freely again.

CHAPTER 15

"And when I crossed Jewell Canyon, I felt a pull on the line. Then I started reeling her in, I saw the bill from that big 'ol marlin come up out of the water. I had to push Maggie away. Yeah, I was enjoying what she was doing, but there was no way in hell I was gonna let that fish go…"

All eyes turned to her.

Some of the fishermen, some as fat and oily as their bait, cracked mischievous smiles while envisioning the very private aspects to her relationship that Mark was describing without a care in the world.

She awoke with a gasp.

"Whoa!" Julian emerged from around the corner. "You alright? Bad dreams?"

Maggie looked at the hotel room she had shared with him. "You can say that." She examined the covers to make sure they were covering her up entirely. Her hands felt along her body, making sure her clothes were still on and searching for any signs of any activity.

She found nothing.

Though she did not think of Julian as a fiend, it was hard for her to imagine sharing a room with someone of his sex without him trying to get a little reward. She could see the scrunches in the couch where he had slept. Truly, he had been there all night—well, from three o'clock onward.

She looked at the clock on her nightstand. It was a few minutes after seven.

Explains why I'm so groggy.

Her eyes went back to Julian. He was showered and dressed for the day, gathering his wallet and phone. It was the activity of a man heading out to work.

"What's going on?" she asked.

"I was able to rent a truck and trailer for the dead shark we found last night," Julian said. "The guy just texted me and said he's almost here. Then I'll be driving it to the Victoria Institute to meet with one of their researchers. Dr. Joanne Malner. I've consulted with her in the past, though only by phone. This'll be my first time working with her in person."

It took Maggie a few moments to realize she was hitting him with an inquisitive stare.

"Oh! Uh, that's nice… you sound excited about that." Sensing that her tone seemed a bit jealous, she decided to shift into a more humorous way of phrasing the statement. "Let me guess: she's hot and you've got a crush on her."

Julian shook his head. "She's sixty-four. Sweet lady, but… no. Just a nice person whom I've enjoyed working with in the past. It's gonna be a good change in pace compared to most of the people I've encountered during this assignment."

Maggie tilted her head. Without even thinking about it, she batted her eyelashes.

"There's at least *one* that isn't so bad, right?"

Julian stiffened like a deer in the headlights.

"Of—of course." He smiled, unsure what else to say to that. *When in doubt, use your wit.* "There's one in particular that makes a hell of a cup of coffee."

Maggie chuckled at that. She reflected on the previous night; particularly the hauling of the shark and their interactions before that.

What was supposed to be a joyous recollection shifted to a moment of embarrassment.

"Oh, Agent Reed…"

"You know you can call me Julian."

"Right, Julian. Listen, about last night, I'm sor—"

"Oh, that." He started putting his boots on. "You know, I thought about it, and I realized how out of touch I probably sounded. I mean, yeah, the basis of my point is true. But it probably wasn't the right time for me to say it. I mean, you're in the middle of your situation. I suppose, sometimes, it's not a bad thing to have a little help."

Maggie felt a warm soothing feeling creep up her body.

"You have nothing to be sorry for," she said. "I'm the bitch. I'm literally sleeping in your bed, and I had the nerve to talk down to you. I'm just…" She sighed. "I'm at rock bottom. I guess I needed to lash out. I just wish it wasn't to the one person who has lent me a helping hand."

"Don't apologize," he said. "You're helping me to solve my case. If you think you're a freeloader, think again."

"I suppose it beats what most men in this town would ask of me in this sort of tradeoff."

Julian read between the lines and nodded.

"Fair enough." He stood up, holstered his service weapon, and went for the door. "I'm off. You gonna be okay here? You can come with me if you wish. I hate to leave you alone if you're worried about people following you."

Maggie gave the offer some thought. It was a nice offer on his part. It was true that she carried a little bit of concern after last night.

The filthy dream replayed in her mind. It was more than a dream, but a terrible memory of a time she felt so embarrassed from Mark telling his buddies about carnal details of a marlin fishing trip he took her on.

That jackass had a way of talking, especially when he was in a good mood. Often, he liked to talk after sex. He had a way of going on and on about things he was proud of, whether it was trash-talking someone, making a big catch, or getting the eye of an attractive woman.

She looked at the clock. 7:05.

If that woman has been sleeping over at his place since I left, it's possible she could be there right now.

An idea crystalized.

It was a long shot, but may yet pay off.

"Actually, can I borrow your truck?"

Julian perked up with a surprised, "Oh!" He dug through his pockets and found the key. "Yeah, I suppose. You're a good driver, right?"

Maggie laughed and extended her hand.

"Your baby's safe with me."

"I wouldn't call it that," he replied. "It belongs to the agency. They'll dock my pay if anything happens to it."

"I'll drive five miles under the limit," she promised. "I just want to check something out today."

Julian looked at his key. If his superiors knew he was letting a civilian drive one of their vehicles, he would never hear the end of it. But there was something about Maggie that was hard to say no to.

"Oh, dear God."

He handed it over to her.

"Thanks!" She got out of bed. "How long do you think you'll be gone?"

"It's about a twenty-five minute drive to the institute," he said. "Beyond that, it all depends on Dr. Malner."

Maggie acknowledged his answer with a nod. "You think it'll lead to an answer that can solve your investigation?"

"It'll help," he said. "But I still need a location for where the hazardous material is being dumped, as well as *who* is doing it—not just the contractor, but the person supplying the material—and, in addition, I need to know *what* it is."

His response finalized Maggie's decision to follow through on her idea. She decided not to tell him what it was. If Julian knew what was on her mind, he would snatch that truck key out of her hand.

She ended the conversation with, "Good luck, then!"

"Thanks." He went for the door, giving her one last glance. "Take care of yourself. I'll see you later."

"Yep. Bye!"

As soon as the door shut behind him, Maggie got out of bed and got changed.

That asshole Mark might be having another round with what's-her-name at this very moment. Once he's satiated, they'll probably talk shop. If I can get in the house, I might overhear something useful. And I know where Mark likes to hide his spare key.

The angel on her shoulder tried to warn her against what she was doing. In typical fashion, Maggie ignored the voice and proceeded.

Dressed in jeans and a black tank top, she tucked Julian's key in her pocket and stepped outside.

CHAPTER 16

Maggie parked the truck a few houses down the street. For a few minutes she watched Mark's house. From where she sat, the lights appeared to be off inside. The garage door was shut, as expected.

She began second-guessing her choice to infiltrate the property. In a way, it felt exciting, as if she was a secret agent gathering intelligence. The fact she was helping out a real life agent gave credence to that thought. Of course, Julian was not a spy. He was just a grunt for the EPA, though better than what he gave himself credit for.

It was refreshing to meet someone who had a passion for something that was not sex or alcohol. Maybe he was lacking in the self-confidence department, but that was not something that bothered her too much. He wasn't lazy and did not have any delusions of grandeur. In a way, his wish for a quiet country life added to his appeal. Maggie had occasionally fantasized of such things herself. She forced such visions from her mind, as they were unobtainable. Secondly, it seemed rather lonely. It was an odd drawback, given her growing disdain for people. But she worried that such peace and quiet would become torturous in itself, as she would have nobody to share her life with.

Oddly enough, that fear was no longer present. Julian seemed to be the type of guy who wouldn't cheat or leave her in the dust. Like her, he was a guy looking for normalcy.

She smacked herself.

Holy shit, Mag. Knock it off. You've known the guy for what? Two days? And here you are entertaining fantasies of running away with him to the woods. Are you insane?

She reminded herself as to why she was here.

Maggie stepped out of the truck and walked up the sidewalk to the house she had lived in for a few years.

Looking at it now, it dawned on her how unhappy she had been. Sure, she was financially taken care of. But Mark didn't care about her, and she knew it. To him, she was a toy to be used for pleasure. And use her, he did. When she did not want to, he would be quick to use the 'who keeps a roof over your head?' card. Then there were the nights he didn't come home and the flirting he openly took part in, even in her presence.

Reflecting on the years, it was obvious Mark was screwing around. Deep down, Maggie always knew, but she convinced herself out of believing it out of fear of losing everything. It was a rational fear, for he truly did strip her of everything she had, including her access to funds.

What are the odds that I run into Julian right after the breakdown with Mark took place?

She tapped herself on the cheek. Julian was front and center on her mind and she couldn't shake him loose.

Maggie, you're damaged goods. He isn't gonna want you anyway. Now, snap out of it.

She arrived at the driveway. Nobody was at the window.

Her heart thumped with increased intensity. What she was about to do was technically breaking and entering, even if it was with the use of a key.

She went to the garage's side door. Farther up along the wall were a few concrete blocks that were hidden by some bushes.

Maggie knelt by the middle block and lifted it up.

The sight of Mark's spare house key brought a smile to her face. That idiot knew she was aware of it. A smarter man would have moved it to a different location. Then again, with all the illegal activity he was taking part in, not to mention the involvement of a client/mistress, he did not have time to think of such trivial matters.

She went to the side door. Sucking in a breath, she inserted the key and unlocked it.

It was real now.

Maggie slowly opened the door. Sure enough, next to Mark's truck was that black Buick Encore the other woman operated.

She slowly shut the door and moved across the garage for the interior door leading into the house. In doing so, she passed the Buick.

A double-take brought her attention to some tan folders that were on her front passenger seat. In addition, there was a briefcase in the back, with a few other tan folders.

Maggie found herself staring at the vehicle.

The woman left it in a garage... she doesn't know anyone can get inside... I wonder if she did not bother to lock her car.

Firstly, Maggie opened the interior door a crack to make sure nobody was on the house's ground level. The room was dark and quiet. In fact, as Maggie predicted, the only noise was coming from upstairs.

Mark was getting his morning 'exercise'.

She carefully latched the door and went to the Buick's passenger side. Her hand slipped over the handle.

Crap, what if this thing has an alarm?

After some hesitation, Maggie decided to take the chance. She had already come this far.

The door opened without a sound, much to Maggie's relief.

Right away, she snatched up one of the tan folders and opened it. Inside was a stack of papers—a manifest. From top to bottom, the page was covered in rectangular columns and rows. On the leftmost column were the names of various materials. Benzene, acetone, DMSO, fipronil, methomyl, mancozeb, phosphate, borane were just the top few rows. In the next column were quantities and dates.

Maggie checked the next folder. Instead of a manifest, she found what appeared to be company documents.

In the corner of the top page was a stamp from *Goliath Industries.*

Maggie thought about it. The name sounded vaguely familiar. She resisted the temptation to look it up on the internet in favor of snooping. Time was of the essence, and if she was caught, the consequences would be dire; moreso, now that she was learning more and more about this woman…

…whose name was Ria Thorne, based on the name on the Buick's insurance and registration papers. That same name was on some of the company documents.

Maggie's phone would still serve a purpose. Instead of getting on the internet, she pulled up the phone's camera app and started snapping images of all of the papers, starting with the manifest. Once she finished sorting through those, she took images of several documents.

Next, she moved to the briefcase in the backseat. It was heavy, as though full of bricks.

In a sense, that's exactly what was inside—bricks of cash.

"Damn!"

She snapped an image of the cash, then shut the briefcase. Like a police officer investigating a crime scene, she took an image of the vehicle's license plate and VIN number. For the latter, she opened the center console again to get another look at the registration.

Inside was another hidden gem. A phone.

Maggie picked it up and tapped the screen. To her delight, the menu screen lit right up.

That dumb woman Ria Thorne really was careless. This was a business phone, based on the contacts and text messages.

She went through the list of text chats.

First, there was someone by the name of R. Tarby. Based on the interactions, he was an individual of authority. Ria was very apologetic in the text history and eager to please.

We have new materials coming on the 22nd. Make sure the contractors are available. And what of the agency?

There's only one agent, but he's being a real pain.

Make sure your people are not caught. If they go down, they could bring us down with them.

I'm doing my best.

Maggie checked some other conversations. Right away, she recognized her ex-boyfriend's name.

She clicked on the text and saw her most recent message thread with Mark. It took place late yesterday afternoon, starting with Ria asking, *Are you sure you can't dump in a different location?*

He responded, *The Darling Ravine is the best place. Otherwise, I'm going to have to go hundreds of miles out into the Gulf. I'm not interested in cutting through shipping lanes and Coast Guard patrol zones with barrels of your slop on deck.*

Maggie used her phone and snapped images of the conversation.

This little mission proved fruitful. She had a name to the company as well as their representative buttering up local fishermen to do their dirty work. Better yet, she had a list of the hazardous material.

The only downside was *how* she obtained this information. Maggie was not an expert in law, but she was aware that if evidence was obtained in a sketchy manner, such as sneaking into somebody's house without permission, it could be thrown out in trial.

Regardless, Julian had something to work with. At the very least, he would be able to locate the dump site and get more agents in the area.

She heard the sound of footsteps coming down the stairs.

"Shit."

Instinctively, she slammed Ria's passenger door.

"*Shit!*"

Realizing she easily could have been heard, she went for the exit. Once outside the garage, she made a run for Julian's truck, all the while praying that Mark and Ria did not notice.

***

"I'm telling you, Mark, I heard a door slam," Ria said. She tied her robe around herself and moved to the garage.

Mark went to the front window and peeked outside. In the early morning quiet, his ex-flame Maggie Pine stuck out like a sore thumb. What was more interesting was the vehicle she was using. He had seen it before. After some thought, he realized it was the truck used by the EPA agent.

"Son of a bitch."

"That's the word!" Ria exclaimed.

Mark went into the garage. "What's the matter?"

"What do you think?" Ria said, holding up her phone with the text conversation still on the screen.

"You left your car unlocked?"

"I was in your garage!" Ria said. "You keep your *garage* unlocked?!"

"Never," he said. "I always lock it."

"You sure about that? It doesn't look like anyone broke in," Ria growled.

"No, I swear, I—" Mark put a hand on his forehead. "Shit! The spare key! I forgot it was even there…"

"Oh, *wonderful*." Ria began to pace nervously. "Who knows what she knows."

"Are all the papers there?"

"Yes, but in case you've forgotten, we live in the 21st century, where people can take all sorts of images with a little rectangular device that looks like *this*!" She held up her smartphone.

"Good point."

Ria tossed her phone into the car and slammed the door shut. "What the hell are we going to do? My boss will kill me if anything comes from this."

Mark lifted his own phone. "It's alright. I have just the guy for the job… for the right price, that is."

Ria glared at him. "You do realize, if my company goes down, *you* go down as well, right? I mean, they'll figure out you're one of the people I've been contracting with."

"Yeah, I know… wait…" Mark looked her in the eye. "*One* of the contractors? Who else have you hired?"

Ria groaned. "Isaac Crogen."

Mark's throat tightened. "Oh. I didn't know. I just thought…" He cleared his throat. "Have you used the same 'negotiation tactics' with him as you have with me, by any chance? Or…"

Ria squeezed her eyes shut. "I'll give you an extra thirty grand. Just take care of the issue, will ya? And quietly! I can't emphasize that last part enough."

"Sure." Mark stared at her for several more seconds, hoping to satisfy his curiosity about the Crogen situation. A red-hot look from her got him to focus on the task at hand. He went through his contacts and made the call. "Good morning, Glenn. You up for a little bonus money?... Good, because you need to act fast…"

CHAPTER 17

Dr. Joanne Malner was considered by all to be a happy, upbeat woman. There was a motherly quality about her that everyone on her floor found endearing. For many, she was the one to bounce ideas or concerns off of when they were going through a rough patch in life. In essence, she was a shining star in the institute.

At least once a week, she brought donuts and coffee into the institute for all the staff on her floor to enjoy.

Julian was unaware of that last fact until his arrival. He was greeted personally by Dr. Malner and led to the laboratory where the necropsy would take place. While the specimen was being transferred, the doctor insisted he have himself a donut and a cup of hot joe.

The agent was not going to say no to that.

"Oh, the things I do for my country," he quipped in response to her offer. After some more small talk, Dr. Malner got down to business. She went to work in the lab, leaving Julian to wait in the lobby to enjoy the refreshments.

Half an hour later, he was called into the lab.

When he saw Dr. Malner this time, she was void of her usual cheerful smile. She appeared exhausted and completely baffled. Right away, he attributed some of that to the horrendous smell in the lab. Air freshener and ventilation systems did their best to combat it, but overall, it was as though the two of them were standing in the middle of a haunted bog where many corpses lay rotting.

"Agent Reed, I hope you're ready, because this is one for *Sherlock Holmes.*"

Julian looked at the body lying on the cadaver table. The twelve-foot shark had been sliced open across its belly, allowing access to its stomach tissue and other internal organs. Its head had been stitched shut following an examination of the brain tissue. X-rays of its cartilage skeleton were hung up on the walls for observation.

Julian was not so much looking at them, but the green substance pooling on the table. Much of it came from its bloodstream as well as the pores on its snout.

"What the hell happened to it?" he asked.

Dr. Malner put her hands to the side and shook her head. "Where to begin?" She picked up a vial of the green fluid. "Over the years, scientists have discovered the effects of chemical waste on living organisms in vitro. Several classes of environmental chemicals, like arsenic, chromium, methylmercury, and many others are exogenous influencers that can change genome function."

"Give it to me straight, Doctor," Julian said, anticipating a longwinded explanation full of mumbo jumbo he was not going to understand nor remember. "Give it to me straight as though I'm eight years old. What happened to this shark?"

Malner breathed through her facemask, which she still kept on for its miniscule effect of blocking the smell. Miniscule was better than nothing.

"Basically, while this fish was in gestation, it was exposed to a variety of toxins that essentially transformed its biology while it was still an embryo."

"So, it was exposed while its mother was pregnant with it," Julian surmised. "Meaning, she must have ingested some not-so-good material."

"In a nutshell, yes," Dr. Malner said.

"Would she have been mutated as well?"

Malner shook her head. "Not in a way she would have survived. She probably was terminally ill for a long time. Obviously, she had to have lived long enough to give birth. That's not the scariest part."

She pulled up a chart that displayed all sorts of readings taken from the fish's blood.

"What am I looking at?" Julian asked.

"There are traces of many different pollutants in its system, plus a few markers I don't quite recognize. Given the examination of its Ampullae of Lorenzini, I think I know why I don't recognize them." She picked up another vial full of light-green fluid. There were at least four of them stored together on a plastic tray.

Julian remembered the burns on the hull of his boat while the thing was attacking.

"Acid?"

"A very strong acid," she said. "Highly corrosive. You're lucky it didn't get too much on your boat, or you'd be lying on the bottom of the sea right now."

It was only eight-thirty in the morning and Julian was already needing an aspirin. "How the hell could this thing possibly survive this? I mean, these alterations to its biology are so extreme, I don't understand how it could function."

"For most of its short existence, it probably wished it *was* dead," Malner replied. "I was able to examine the brain. There is considerable swelling around the pain center. This thing was living in agony twenty-four-seven. Have you ever experienced nerve pain?"

"A little bit of sciatica," Julian said.

"Imagine that, but severe, and never-ending. You know what that could do to a living thing? Especially a predator?"

Julian reflected on the time he had a minor back injury which caused some swelling, resulting in some compressed nerves. After a day, he was short-tempered and restless.

And that was a relatively minor experience for a short term.

"It made it highly aggressive," he said.

"Yes. Pain in both animals and humans can trigger a sort of fight-or-flight response. Since it can't swim away from the pain, it leans towards the 'fight' part. You said during our phone call that it attacked your vessel?"

"Correct," Julian said.

"This thing would've attacked a freight ship if given the chance," Malner continued. "Actually, I'm grateful it didn't. The acid secreting from its pores would gradually melt through the hull and cause water to flood the lower decks." She whistled at the scary thought. "Could you imagine?"

Julian was in thought. His mind returned to the night he and Maggie discovered Willy Phelps' boat.

THAT'S why there were chemical burns on his boat!

"Here's a question: how is it the shark doesn't get melted away by its own acid supply? I mean, we're talking about something that's strong enough to burn through metal. Wouldn't it just melt through the shark's body?"

"The same could be said about our own stomach acid," Dr. Malner replied. "Many people don't realize how strong it is. But our stomach tissues are designed to withstand the acid. The same can be said of the sack where the shark's acid is stored."

She directed Julian to another table where tissue samples of the shark were being stored.

"But, to your point, should our stomach contents spill into the rest of our body, there'd be serious problems. As I mentioned, our bellies are designed to keep the stuff contained. The same can be said for the shark's acid sack."

Malner lifted a vial of the acid and gently poured a tiny amount on a slab of meat taken from the shark's abdominal region. The flesh wilted like a flower, breaking down to the molecular level.

Julian put a hand over his nose. He had never watched flesh liquify before, let alone smelled it.

"So, even the shark is not immune to its own supply," he surmised.

Dr. Malner called in one of the lab techs to properly dispose of the sample, then took it upon herself to properly secure the rest of the acid.

She brought up an image used by a portable MRI machine. Located above the throat was a hollow area with a large vein leading to a large pore in the shark's snout.

"This is where its sack is located. The shark's body produces acid and rapidly fills this hollow region. When it attacks, it uses muscles in its neck to contract that sack with significant force and sprays its prey."

"Wouldn't that be useless in the water?"

"Actually, it would be most *useful* in the water," the doctor said. "In the water, it would act in a way similar to an octopus jetting ink. Only, instead of masking its escape, it would burn the eyes and fins of an animal it intends to eat. The effect would be quickly diluted by the water, but that's the point. The shark can't really eat something that's melted to the bone. You should be grateful it's only a baby. The amount of acid it produced was considerably minor. A larger shark, on the other hand, might produce the stuff more rapidly. Worse, it can jet it out in huge streams. Like I said before, it's highly aggressive due to the unimaginable pain it exists in. Anything it comes across, it'll kill."

Looking at the dead fish, Julian was starting to regret eating those donuts. The smell continued assaulting him, seemingly growing more intense while he comprehended the ramifications of the shark's mutation.

Damn! Thank God this thing wasn't any bigger. It would...

He stopped mid-thought, recalling one specific phrasing of a sentence in the doctor's report.

"For most of its short existence, it probably wished it was dead."

"How old would you say this shark is? I mean, it's twelve feet long. I imagine it's an adult blue shark, right?"

Malner referred to an item on the chart.

Nutropin.

"Examination of the reproductive organs revealed that this shark is maybe a few months old."

Julian tilted forward. "A few months?"

The doctor nodded. She knew how insane she sounded. At the same time, she also knew she was correct.

"Among other contaminants I discovered in its system, there was a considerable amount of growth hormone. This shark's mother had a toxic smorgasbord to say the least. It killed her and mutated him."

"So, if this thing survived for another few months, it could potentially…" Julian paused, feeling foolish for even having this conversation in a context that was not humorous. "How big could this thing have gotten?"

Dr. Malner looked at the fish and sighed. "I cannot say for sure, but if I had to make an educated guess, I think this thing was capable of reaching a length of forty feet, at least."

Julian leaned against the wall. The thought of a forty-plus-foot toxic shark lurking in the water was too much to comprehend.

"Thank God it's dead," he said aloud to himself. "Who knows what kind of damage this creature may have caused."

"Keep in mind, you discovered this one by accident," Malner said. "How do we know there aren't any others?"

Julian remained against the wall, detesting the logic the doctor was using. He knew she was correct, but so badly wanted to bask in the comfort of his assumption that the horror was over.

"I suppose, if there is another one of these sharks swimming around out there, it'll eventually reveal itself."

Almost in direct response to that statement, one of the lab techs entered the lab. "Agent Reed? You're with the EPA, right?"

"I am."

"Maybe you're already aware, but have you seen the news?" He pointed into the lobby, where a television broadcast was on screen.

Julian and Dr. Malner stepped into the lounge to get a look for themselves. On the screen was helicopter footage of several police and fire-rescue vehicles on the northwest shore of Pelican Grove.

On the bar at the bottom of the screen was text which read *Chemical Explosion off the shore of Pelican Grove, Florida.*

The news went to a brief interview with Sheriff Gillis. He wore sunglasses and looked as annoyed as ever, probably only entertaining an interview in exchange for the press to go away.

"Sheriff, is it true one of the victims on the beach was found literally burnt to the bone?"

"I cannot comment on that matter."

"But the explosion? There have been reports of chemical drums aboard that vessel. Can you tell us who it belongs to?"

"I can't comment on that either. Now, if you'll excuse me..."

He turned and walked away.

"Son of a bitch," Julian muttered.

The news anchor continued reading his script, starting with, *"According to local sources, the explosion happened at three in the morning. We're still waiting on the names of the victims..."*

Julian cursed under his breath. Now, there was no doubt the incident was caused by a different shark.

He turned to look at Dr. Malner. "That acid the creature emits; could it combust if mixed with other chemical products?"

The doctor nodded. "I don't know what was on that boat, but to answer your question, yes. It could easily trigger an explosion."

Julian went for the door. "Thank you, Doctor. Pardon me, but I have to leave right away."

Dr. Malner offered a wave. "Good luck, Agent."

Thanks. I'm gonna need it.

CHAPTER 18

It was ten minutes to eight when Maggie returned to the hotel room. She rested on the bed, sorting through the photographs she had taken of Ria Thorne's materials. The list of all the materials the company was trying to get rid of made her stomach knot up.

A *Google* search of the company Goliath Industries produced a myriad of results. From top to bottom, she found articles talking about the ups and downs in the company's history. They were a manufacturer of home health products and food production, with ambitions to create their own brand of over-the-counter medications.

Its CEO, Reno Tarby, started his fortune with the ownership of a scrapyard. In 2017, his facility in northern California was fined ten-thousand dollars for improper labeling and storage of hazardous materials. Two years later, a specialty chemical plant in Texas was caught attempting to improperly bury waste in an abandoned mine. As a result, the plant was permanently shut down and Reno Tarby was subject to investigation.

Over the years since then, there had been numerous allegations surrounding Goliath Industries and its CEO and founder, Reno Tarby. In addition to the reports of poor working conditions, the company faced allegations of going after reporters.

In 2021, an independent journalist named Hanna Urn published four articles in the course of a month, detailing some undercover work at one of their food plants. There, she revealed how cows, chickens, pigs, and several other livestock were living neck-to-neck with one another. Thc photos revealed animals covered in their own feces and dramatically overweight due to a poor grain diet.

In late July of that year, Hanna Urn died after reportedly falling asleep at the wheel and hitting a semi-truck head-on.

In 2022, another journalist by the name of Toby Becker was found dead as a result of a drug overdose. Friends and family contested the claims, stating that Toby never even drank alcohol or used tobacco, let alone used narcotics. Prior to his death, he was investigating the disappearance of a man who worked at one of Goliath's recycling centers. According to Toby's blog, the man was interested in going public regarding sexual scandals involving the CEO.

Maggie reclined on the bed and brought up the images of the text messages. The first one showed the list of ongoing conversations. There was Mark's name, Isaac Crogen, R. Tarby, and a few others. Maggie was about to flip to the next image when one particular name suddenly caught her eye.

Gillis.

Maggie sat up straight. "How did I miss that before?"

No wonder the sheriff was eager to interfere with Julian's investigation. He was on Goliath's payroll. She never held a high opinion of the guy. Nobody did, really. The fact he would take money probably meant he was heading for early retirement. It was no secret that he didn't care for his job. The only reason he ran for sheriff was because he wanted to run the show. It had nothing to do with responsibility and protecting the public. As sheriff of this county, he hardly answered to anyone. Only a small percentage of the population bothered voting in the local elections. Most of those who did only voted for the most familiar name, which was his.

She was tempted to give Julian a call. Though he had nothing kind to say about Gillis, Julian was the type to play nice and not step on anybody's toes. If he found anything significant, of course he would run it by the sheriff. It was one-sided professional courtesy.

Then there was the issue of safety. Goliath Industries were clearly unafraid to use violent means to dispose of people they found troublesome. Logically, if they were paying off the head of law enforcement in Pelican Grove, it came with the caveat that he would have to dispose of any threat. Up until now, Julian's position as an EPA agent granted him some level of protection. A dead agent would only draw more unwanted attention, not just from the EPA, but also from other agencies.

That protection would be moot if Julian discovered too much.

With that in mind, she chose to make the call. Maggie stood up and went to the window for the best cell signal. Looking out into the parking lot, she hoped to see his rental truck and trailer. She really wanted him back here.

What she saw instead was a grey utility van with part of its front bumper hanging low.

Maggie lowered her phone.

Wait... is that Glenn?

The van parked in a space. Its driver's side door opened.

Out came a heavily built man with tattoos covering both arms and a scowl on his face. He strutted right for the hotel's main entrance.

"Oh, God."

Maggie's first instinct was to dial 9-1-1. She stopped herself, knowing the Sheriff's Department would be the first to respond. If Gillis was corrupt, it was safe to assume many, if not all, of his deputies were as well. Calling them would only help Glenn's cause.

She needed to run.

After grabbing her belongings, she went into the hallway and started to run down the nearest stairwell in hopes of escaping through a back exit.

The horrid sound of a man being strangled at the check-in counter stopped her in her tracks.

"Maybe now you'll be willing to answer. Which room is the agent staying in?"

There was the sound of a man's head being bashed against a desk.

"Last chance."

Whimpering, the clerk replied, "Second floor. Room two-twelve."

"Good. Don't bother making any more phone calls. You wanna stay in one piece? Sit behind your desk and pretend nothing's going on." Glenn threw him across the room and marched for the stairwell.

Maggie clenched her teeth. "Shit!"

She could not get down there without passing him. There was no choice now but to retreat to her room. Perhaps she would be able to get out through a fire escape.

More importantly, she needed to alert Julian.

She entered their room, locked the door, and started dialing his number.

***

When Julian arrived at the beach, most of the crowd he had seen in the television footage was gone. There were a few nosey locals in the area, watching things play out. Aside from them, only the sheriff and some other first responders were present.

Gillis did not hide his displeasure at Julian's arrival, neither in face nor voice. The agent had barely stepped out of the truck when he was greeted with, "What the hell are you doing here?"

Julian moved under the caution tape and laid eyes on the beach. That smell from the mutated blue shark had also permeated the air here. Washing up on shore were thick green globs of secretion identical to the waste secreted by the shark's gills, except there was a lot of it.

"Sheriff, the situation is worse than we thought."

Gillis' face wrinkled. "Yeah. Five people are dead."

Julian turned his eyes to the tornado of smoke wafting a half-mile offshore. "You mean to tell me there was an attack on that boat *and* here on the beach?"

Gillis checked a text on his phone.

Then Julian witnessed something more strange than killer acid-spitting sharks; the Sheriff's demeanor changed to something pleasant.

He tucked his phone away and spoke in a professional, courteous manner.

"We don't know the cause of the accident just yet. However, sir, we would appreciate your help. I'm aware you have some underwater drones at your disposal. Would you be willing to take a ride out with us? Out to the wreck, that is? Some of the evidence might be lying on the seabed, and considering the risk of chemical hazards, I would prefer to send a machine rather than risk the safety of a diving team."

Julian was taken aback. The Sheriff's attitude was an unexpected one. On top of that, there was the drastic shift in his demeanor—almost as if he had read something on a text that gave him incentive to tone down the abrasiveness.

Whatever the case was, Julian agreed with the base point.

"Absolutely, I'll be glad to help. But Sheriff, there's one other thing. You're going to think I'm crazy, but I promise you I have evidence to back this up."

Julian pulled out his phone and allowed Gillis to see photos of the dead shark.

"You killed a shark?"

"It attacked my boat last night," Julian said. "This thing has had its entire chromosome structure screwed up beyond recognition because of whatever's being dumped out there. Contact Dr. Malner at the Victoria Institute. She'll be able to substantiate my findings."

"How does that relate to this?" he asked.

Julian pointed at the slime accumulating on the beach. "You see all this crap? This is building up in their bodies like snot, and being expelled. The shark that attacked the people on this beach was loaded with it."

Gillis handed the phone back. "I don't know, Agent. That seems a little far-fetched."

"Yeah? As far fetched as a random chemical spill here on the beach?" the agent replied. "And what was on that boat that exploded? There are reports stating there were large drums on its deck."

"Might've been fuel," Gillis said. "A lot of boats take spare fuel when going on long voyages."

"Or, they were dumping something out there."

Gillis stood quietly, his eyes on the water. He was deep in thought in a way that a man was when trying to invent a solution to a problem.

"Okay. In that event, ride out with me. Bring your drone. The only way to find out is to get a better view of the wreckage."

Julian could not argue with that.

"Okay. I'll come out with you. But I recommend you have a bunch of guns aboard. If I'm right about there being a shark out there, it's *big* and *highly* dangerous. I'm talking about a real sea monster."

He watched the Sheriff's face. The guy did not seem all that surprised at all to hear this mumbo-jumbo about a giant mutant shark. There was some mild confusion, but it came off as a performance rather than genuine.

"Okay, that's what we'll do," Gillis said.

Julian's phone vibrated in his hand. He looked down and recognized the number Maggie had dialed into it.

"Excuse me for a moment." He stepped away and answered the call. "Hey, Maggie. What's going on?"

"Julian! Stay away from the sheriff!"

"Beg your pardon?"

"Don't meet with Gillis under any circumstances. He's working for THEM!"

Julian sensed the fright in her voice and the sounds of fast-paced motion. She did not just sound like someone who was scared, but someone who was moving with haste.

"Are you alright?"

"Julian... Glenn is here at the hotel. He's in the hall. He knows what room we're in. He practically strangled the clerk to death trying to figure out where we are. Julian, I think he's here to kill me."

"Okay, I'm coming. I'll get ahold of—"

"Julian, the Sheriff's Department is compromised. How do we know any deputies that are sent in an emergency call aren't also on the company's payroll?"

Based on the way she spoke, she had discovered something. Whatever it was, it was the reason she asked to borrow his truck. The idea probably was to be discreet, since her rusty vehicle stood out like a sore thumb, even in this town. If that was the case, she failed to realize that his vehicle was also easily recognizable, especially to those who resented his very presence.

If Glenn saw her driving the vehicle, he was able to figure out she was staying with him. Whatever she discovered, it was enough for Glenn to go after her with murderous intent.

"Okay, I'm on my way."

"Please hurry."

Julian went to the rental truck.

"What's the matter?" Sheriff Gillis called to him.

"Uh… The drone is back at the hotel. I need to grab it. I'll be back." He got in the driver's seat and did a U-turn.

Sheriff Gillis watched the agent disappear into the distance. He had worked in this profession long enough to know a lie when he heard one. It was part of the trade to deal with liars, and in Gillis' case, to lie himself.

His phone rang.

On the screen was the name Thorne. It was the second time she had called him that morning.

"Yes?"

"How's it going over there, Sheriff?"

"Just dandy."

She did not appreciate the sarcasm in his voice. *"What's the situation with the agent?"*

"He had to go somewhere. He says he'll be back, but I'm not sure he will. I think he smells a rat."

He heard her groan on the other end of the line.

"He's making my boss nervous. I want him taken care of NOW."

"I'm aware. But it's not like I can just take him around the corner and whack him. Not unless we want the entire agency crawling around here. We need to be extra discreet in how we handle this. If we get him on the water, we can claim he was attacked by a shark. But we need to catch him on the water for that to work."

"You sure he won't ride out with you?"

"I can't say for sure. But I know this; he's getting increasingly desperate. He's bound to go out again to search for that shit you're putting in the water."

"Speaking of the shark, are you handling it?"

Gillis exhaled slowly. It was one more thing he had to deal with. He focused on the cash coming his way.

This incident on the beach was not the first sign of a large shark in the area. Yesterday, the remains of a small cruiser were discovered. On its flying bridge was a large tooth covered in green slime. In addition, the hull was covered in acid burns that caused it to sink.

Between that, Willy Phelps' boat, and last night's disappearances, Gillis was willing to accept that something unnatural had occurred. There indeed was a giant shark in the water, and it was physically altered by leaking chemical drums. As long as it was out there, it was going to draw unwanted attention.

"I'm handling it right now. Bear with me."

"Handle it fast, because all our asses are on the line."

"Yes, lady."

"Don't 'lady' me, Sheriff. I'm gonna be coming out there shortly to oversee the disposal of the last of the barrels. I want to get a look at the dump site myself, that way I can assure my boss none of it can be found."

"Understood." He hung up and grumbled while dialing another number. "Bitch." He made the call and lifted the phone to his ear.

"Yes, Sheriff?"

"Hi, Paul. You and your friends feel like making some extra cash?"

"Fuck yeah!"

"Good. Make sure you bring rifles and shotguns. You're gonna need 'em."

CHAPTER 19

Maggie pushed the sofa against the door, then jammed the dining table and chairs against it. The door was made mostly from metal and had an electronic lock. Between that and the barricade, she was certain she would be safe.

She hurried to the window and looked for a latch, only to find none existed. Not that it mattered—there was no fire escape on the outside of the building.

Maggie slapped the window. "Damn it!"

She heard the door handle twisting. Putting her back to the window, Maggie held a lamp to use as a club.

Okay. Just relax. He can't get in. The guy would have to possess herculean strength to break that door down.

BEEP!

Maggie's heart skipped a beat. That was the sound of a key card unlocking the door.

"Oh, Lord…"

Only now did it occur to her that Glenn would have demanded a spare key card from the clerk.

Glenn shoved the door open, inching the couch, table, and chairs back. Maggie ran to the barricade and pushed against it.

The intruder hardly budged. He put all of his weight into the door, his tattoo-covered arms bulging as he slowly overcame her defenses.

Inch by inch, the door opened, sliding the sofa and Maggie backwards. Glenn worked on his leverage, putting his left shoulder through the newly-opened gap between the door and the frame. His stone-cold eyes looked at her. He gave little expression other than the strain of the physical force required to get into the room.

Maggie, in contrast, was animated with intense fear. She pushed her feet against the floor, but could not overcome the machine-like force of the ex-con.

"Get out!"

There was no compassion or even delight in his eyes. The guy practically was a machine. All that mattered was fulfilling his objective, which was to break her neck and permanently silence her.

The barricades moved back another six inches, allowing the human monster to wedge himself farther into the opening.

Maggie's eyes began to well. She did not want to die like this. Not strangled and with her skull crushed. She wanted to grow old and live the rest of her life peacefully. *Far* from Pelican Grove, with someone to share the years with.

She closed her eyes.

All she could think about was Julian.

Oh, stop! You're about to get murdered, and you're still hung up on this rebound attraction?

Maggie opened her eyes.

It wasn't a rebound. It was something she'd wanted all of her life; it just didn't have a face until now. For years, she did not think she was worthy of such a good man. Only in the last day did that opinion change. Julian did not make her feel like an item. She felt like a person in his presence, complete with a heart, soul, and worth.

And she knew in her heart that he was coming to her rescue.

Glenn widened the gap.

Maggie abandoned the attempt to keep him out and retreated to the back window. She picked the lamp back up and held it over her shoulder like a tennis racket.

Glenn gave the door one more shove, pushing everything back. He stopped for a moment to take a breath. It had less to do with fatigue and more with letting his victim swell with fear and anticipation. Though his face was emotionless, there was no doubt in Maggie's mind that he was enjoying every minute of this.

A black L-shaped object emerged from behind Glenn. At once, he and Maggie recognized the object that was touching the back of his head.

A pistol.

"Back up. Slowly," Julian said.

Maggie put a hand over her heart. "Oh, thank you, God."

Glenn remained in place, his frustration finally revealing some emotion. He put his hands up and slowly backed into the hallway.

Maggie moved past her makeshift barricade and watched the arrest from the door.

"You alright?" Julian said to her.

"I'm good. Be careful. Glenn's got something up his sleeve, I know it."

Julian kept his gun on the back of his head. "I've got him under control. Isn't that right, Glenn?"

The convict sported a smile.

Julian felt along his belt in search of his cuffs. "Get on your knees and put your hands behind your back."

Glenn slid one foot back and lowered himself to one knee, hands still above his shoulders.

"Stop dragging this out," Julian said.

Finally, the perp spoke.

"Okay."

He sprang off his front foot, ramming his body against Julian's. The pistol was knocked to the side and discharged two rounds uselessly into the wall.

Glenn butted the agent in the face with the back of his head, stunning him long enough for the ex-con to turn around and go for the gun.

Powerful hands closed over Julian's wrist and began twisting. Julian shrieked, the nerves in his hand lighting up like fireworks. His grip on the pistol was quickly deteriorating in spite of his willpower.

He punched Glenn across the chin with his other arm. The convict's head whipped to the side, only to turn back to face him. Julian struck again. He may as well have been punching iron. The large, tattooed man was hardly fazed.

Glenn tilted his head back, then lunged forward, headbutting the agent in the face. Julian's vision turned into fog.

He could feel the criminal grasp the gun by the barrel. In five seconds, it would be pried from his hand.

Julian resorted to one desperate measure.

His thumb pressed down on the magazine eject button, ridding the pistol of its remaining fourteen bullets. A squeeze of the trigger sent the one in the tube through the ceiling.

The weapon was now useless to either combatant.

Glenn, no longer focused on obtaining the gun, resorted to brute force. For the next ten seconds, Julian learned what it felt like to be a punching bag. Fists rammed into his ribcage and face with remarkable speed. Blinded by pain, Julian threw a clumsy haymaker in retaliation.

The convict deflected his arm, forced it downward, and hit the agent across the face with a haymaker of his own.

Julian spun on his feet and hit the floor.

Blood and spit shot from his mouth as Glenn planted a knee on his middle, blowing his air out and pinning him down. Both hands moved to the agent's throat.

Julian kicked his feet, his airway blocked off. His hands grabbed at Glenn's, but failed to pry them off. The fog in his vision thickened and his strength plummeted.

Glenn was practically motionless, watching his enemy with perfectly still eyes while he strangled the life out of him.

Maggie felt an agonizing fear in her soul. It was a fear that far surpassed what she felt inside the hotel room when she thought her life was about to end. For the first time in her life, she feared for the loss of another human being.

She could not let it happen.

She *would* not let it happen. Even if the cost was her own life.

Raising the lamp, she charged at Glenn. Like a gavel, she brought it down hard on the back of his head.

The convict juddered, then looked over at her. The hit was barely an inconvenience.

She struck again, achieving the same result.

Mildly annoyed, Glenn backhanded her across the jaw. Maggie fell against the wall, spilling tears, not from pain, but helplessness. Julian was dying right in front of her, and she was helpless to do anything but watch.

No matter what she did, she failed.

Just like in life.

She lowered her head. It seemed she was made to exist at rock bottom. She had no job, no future, and the one thing she clung to, the one person she felt anything for, was about to be stripped from her.

The lamp dropped from her hand. The shade detached, revealing the yellow bulb inside.

Maggie looked at the round piece of glass.

Like a guardian angel, she heard Julian's voice in her mind.

There's always a way out of a bad situation. Sometimes, things seem completely helpless. In those moments, you've got to keep your head up, because often, the answer is right in front of you.

In her case, it was by her side.

Maggie removed the bulb and held it in her left hand like a softball. She sprang to her feet and charged at Glenn.

With a powerful swing, she smashed the bulb over his left eye.

The convict's mechanical exterior was shattered along with the bulb. He reeled backward, yelling in pain, pressing both hands to his bloody face.

"My eye! My eye! You bitch! Agh! I'm gonna kill you!"

To make good on that promise, he got to his feet.

Julian, gasping for breath, righted himself. He pulled his expandable baton from his belt and went at the wild animal in front of him. A whack across the face stopped Glenn's assault short.

He struck a second time, removing some teeth from the convict's jaw. A kick to the groin and a whack to the forehead dropped Glenn to one knee.

It was Maggie who struck the final blow. She picked Julian's empty pistol up off the floor and struck her attacker right between the eyes.

An unconscious Glenn fell flat on his back.

Exhausted, Julian put his back to the wall.

Maggie ran over to him and put a hand on his face. "Julian, are you okay?"

"Better than him," he quipped. "What about you? Did he hurt you?"

"No, I'm alright," she said. "I'm worried about you, though. You're bleeding."

"No, I'm good. I promise."

She smiled. "You better keep your promise."

Maggie cupped her other hand over his face and pulled him in for a kiss. Julian's eyes widened with surprise. This was not the thanks he was expecting, but it was welcome all the same.

Slowly, he put his arms around her and cemented the embrace.

Several kisses were exchanged, each one elevating in intensity and passion.

A groan from a stirring Glenn brought them back to the situation at hand.

"I better cuff this guy before he wakes up." Julian rolled him to his back and secured the cuffs.

Maggie stepped into the room and returned with some torn fabric from the curtain. "I'm not taking any chances."

She went to work tying his ankles together.

Julian, being the decent human that he was, took some time to wrap a bandage over Glenn's eye. Glass shards stuck out of his socket. He was going to require a surgeon's help to get the fragments removed.

"I'll call an ambulance for this guy."

"But the Sheriff's Department will get notified," Maggie said.

"Not if I call one from outside the county. I'll give the State Police a tip as well. Something tells me the clerk downstairs won't mind helping us out. Especially after getting strangled."

Maggie smiled. "I'd say so."

Julian collected his gun and bullets, and went into the room. "So, what's going on, Maggie? Why'd he come after you? I mean, this was more than tailing you with the hopes of taking you out without anyone noticing. He was about to murder you in broad daylight. I imagine you discovered something that has somebody very, *very* concerned."

Maggie picked up her phone, brought up the images, and handed it to the agent. "Mark's working for Goliath Industries. The lady he's seeing is Ria Thorne. She's one of their representatives, and as it turns out, she's willing to use all her assets to get the job done."

Julian looked at the list of text conversations, seeing Gillis' name in one of the columns. "Son of a bitch."

"Yeah. He's on their payroll."

Julian inhaled deeply through his nose. A vein began to bulge from his forehead.

"They're ready to take us out to keep their operation quiet. Obviously, you were seen while you were obtaining this—How *did* you get this info, by the way?"

Maggie beamed with joy. "I remembered where Mark left his spare key. Better yet, I know his habits. I predicted Ria would still be there if she was spending the night with him regularly. She was. I was able to get a look at everything while they were still fumbling about upstairs."

Julian batted his eyebrows. "Nice."

"Except, I had to leave in a hurry," she said. "I heard them coming down the stairs. They must've known it was me, because while I was waiting here… well, you know the rest of the story." She tilted her head to where Glenn was lying down.

"They're desperate," Julian said. "The sheriff was inviting me to take a ride offshore on his boat."

Maggie put a hand over her mouth. It was not difficult to put the pieces together. In true mafia fashion, they were going to off Julian far from shore and let him sleep with the fishes.

"What do we do?" she asked.

Julian looked at the images of Ria Thorne's conversation with Mark Wall. "The Darling Ravine. Charming name."

"That's where he's been dumping his crap," Maggie said.

"Good. All we need to do now is get out there, get some footage with my drone, and then we'll have a swarm of agents out here. Not to mention the Coast Guard."

Maggie grabbed a jacket. "Then let's get to it."

Julian looked at her with admiration. "Nice work, Maggie. You made my job easy. You ought to be on the payroll. I wish there was something I could do in return."

She leaned against the wall and graced him with a smile. "You could kiss me."

It was a wish Julian was more than happy to grant. For once, there was something in this town that was worth his while.

CHAPTER 20

Paul Relan captain of the trawling vessel *Great Barrier Chief*, took in the powerful smell of chum. On the aft deck of his vessel, his two deckhands, Harold and Moody, prepped for the arrival of their objective.

A cigarette, burnt to the butt, dangled between Moody's teeth as he shoved the scoop into the large tub. The brown mixture of oil, blood, and fish parts hit the water, joining a long line that stretched a quarter-mile southeast. His white tank top was already stained as though he was working on an oil pipeline.

Harold was readying the nets. He had them lifted over the transom, ready to be dropped at any moment. The idea was to find the shark on the fish-finder, get it to swim under the boat, and have it fly right into the net. Afterwards, they would hoist the entangled shark to the surface and shoot the living hell out of it.

Each of the crewmen brought their own weapons aboard for the hunt. Paul brought a double-barrel shotgun, which rested up on the flying bridge with him. Harold brought a pump-action shotgun and a hand pistol.

Then there was Moody. The guy had a tendency to go overboard—literally, in some cases. He brought aboard a bolt-action Remington rifle and a large black case full of dynamite.

Paul was not going to ask where he got it. The answer would probably be a lie anyway. All he had to say to the crewman was, "Do not blow up my boat!" To which Moody replied, "Relax! I know what I'm doing! Trust me!"

With great reluctance, the captain took him at his word. To do that, he had to ignore the warning in his gut which screamed, *No, you idiot! Obviously, he DOESN'T know what the hell he's doing.*

He ignored the gut instinct and proceeded driving the boat westward, parallel with two other vessels that had been contracted by the sheriff.

To the right of the *Great Barrier Chief* was the *Gold Star* and the *Ritualist.* The nearest of the two, the *Gold Star*, was piloted by Captain Lon Burnham. He was a man who wore an open checkered shirt and a tattered tank-top underneath it. When Paul saw him at the moment of their departure, it was clear the guy was hungover. Lon's two deckhands, Freddy and Taggert, were not much better. On at least one occasion, one of them heaved over the side of the boat. Paul surmised that the smell of their chum supply put his nausea over the edge.

A hundred feet or so starboard of the *Gold Star* was the *Ritualist*. Its captain's name was Arthur Faraday. He, too, had two deckhands aboard his vessel. Buggy was blasting music from his radio and bobbing his head to the tunes, while the crewman with a limp, Kal, openly complained about the noise. Between the distance and the music, Paul could not make out what the guy was saying, but the angry tone was plain as day.

It was a sentiment mirrored by Harold. The fisherman grabbed his bolt-action rifle by the barrel and stomped to the starboard side.

"God! I wish I could see that stupid radio from here. I'd put a bullet in the thing and rid us all of the misery. I mean, who blasts disco music like that?"

"I know, right?" Moody replied. "Shark hunting calls for rock 'n roll."

"It could be worse," Paul said to them. "Twelve years ago, I was working on a sword boat. One of the guys was really religious. That in itself wasn't the problem, but the guy had his own radio, and while we were working, he's playing all these hymns. Many of them, I swear, were practically some woman crying while singing. And it was excruciating to listen to."

"Damn!" Moody tossed another scoopful of chum into the ocean. "Anything ever result from that?"

"Can't say," Paul said. "The radio mysteriously disappeared one night. Inexplicable! It was as though someone might've tossed it into the ocean while the guy was sleeping. It was quite the mystery, that's for sure."

The two crewmen chuckled.

"If only someone would do the same for Buggy's radio," Harold said. He climbed up to the flying bridge, scooted past Paul, and went for the boat's radio mic. "*Great Barrier Chief* to *Ritualist.*"

"What's going on, Chief? Got something on the fishfinder?"

"Actually, Arthur, I was gonna ask you to get Buggy to kill that noise. For godsake, listening to that music is like having a sea urchin shoved up my ass."

"There's an image. Okay, let me see what I can do."

Harold looked at Paul. "See what he can do? He's the captain. All he needs to say is 'turn that shit off!'"

"He's too polite," Paul replied.

"It's a no-go, Chief."

Howard lowered his head and tried to make peace with the situation. The next tune echoed from across the sea, obliterating any hope of the fisherman calming his temper.

"Put Kal on the horn, would you please?"

"One sec."

Before long, it was Kal's voice coming through the speaker.

"What is it, Harold?"

"Hi, Kal. Listen, how would you like to make two hundred bucks?"

"Won't say no. What do I need to do to earn it?"

"Take Buggy's radio and toss it overboard. I can't stand listening to that disco crap."

"You know what, Harold? I was thinking of doing it for free, but I wasn't sure if I wanted to deal with the aftermath. But your offer has pushed my willingness over the hump. Keep your ears open."

He left the radio.

The crew of the *Great Barrier Chief* listened in anticipation.

Through the torturous music, they heard Buggy's voice shouting, "Hey! What the hell are you doing? Kal! What the f—"

Splash!

The music vanished instantaneously.

Now, Buggy could be heard clearly. "You piece of shit! I'm gonna kill you!"

"Serves you right," Kal replied. "I was two minutes away from asking the skipper to refund the lady's money and take us home. No amount of cash was worth listening to that shit."

A sound of a struggle and cursing ensued.

Now, those aboard the *Gold Star* were watching the resulting chaos. They held beers in their hands, laughing at the brawl that was taking place between their fellow fishermen.

"Guys! Guys! Guys!" Arthur Faraday shouted. He went to the radio to speak to Harold. *"Hey, Harold! Thanks a lot. See what you started?"*

Harold made sure his laughs were heard through the channel. "Hey, at least this is entertaining, as opposed to the torture being inflicted on all of us."

"Great. And what about me? Goddamnit, guys! Will you knock it off."

Arthur killed his engine in order to deal with his crewmates, causing the other two boats to get ahead of him.

Buggy's voice echoed across the ocean. "You prick! My late mother gave me that radio!"

"*Late* mother?" Kal replied. "Did she stroke out because you made her listen to disco?"

"Motherfucker!"

Aboard the *Great Barrier Chief*, Paul, Harold, and Moody were dying with laughter. It proved contagious, as the three individuals aboard the *Gold Star* were doubling over from laughter. The two groups soon had pains in their stomachs and tears in their eyes.

"I'm gonna break your neck!" Buggy shouted, pinning Kal to the gunnel. The crewman felt himself teetering over the side. Realizing he would not outmuscle Buggy's large girth, he grabbed him by the shirt and let gravity do the rest.

"Here! Let's go find your radio!"

He fell backward, taking Buggy with him.

The dual splashes sparked a fresh wave of obnoxious laughter from the other crews.

Kal and Buggy reemerged on the water's surface, carrying on with their fight. It was well known that the two guys were not exactly drinking buddies. Each day, they tolerated each other's presence in service of the job. Today, that silent tension reached its boiling point, all thanks to Harold's contribution.

Arther was leaning over the side, smacking the gunwale as he shouted to the men to stop.

"I swear, if you guys don't quit, I'll fuck'n use you as shark bait!"

Buggy pushed Kal away. "Not like it would do you any good, Cap. I doubt the shark would like to eat somebody who smells like sauerkraut!"

"Is that right?" Kal replied. "Personally, I think the idea of using your sorry ass as bait is a brilliant idea. That way the shark will choke to death and make the job easier on the rest of us!"

"Oh, you're funny!" Buggy moved with intent to strangle his crewmate. "How would you like if I—"

SPLASH!

Buggy was lifted into the air, arms high, his violent temperament reduced to a babbling mess. Engulfing most of his body were the jaws of an enormous shark. Its front half lifted twenty feet into the air.

Buggy vomited blood as those jaws applied pressure. The fish fell to the side, smashing his head and shoulders against the hull of the *Ritualist*.

"Holy shit!" Arthur shouted.

The boat rocked to port, nearly catapulting him across the deck. Another splash erupted over the starboard side. Rising with the waves was the shark's caudal fin. Like a medieval weapon, it slashed the ship's hull, bending it inward a few inches.

In the water, Kal was kicking and screaming.

To his right came a jet of bloody water, mixed with Buggy's bloated, mashed body. It drifted across Kal's path, the head crushed into the shoulders after its impact with the *Ritualist.*

As he had joked, he was a little too bulky to be swallowed whole.

It was a problem the shark would *not* have with Kal.

He looked over his shoulder just in time to see the mouth coming at him. It closed over his head and shoulders, penetrating many serrated teeth through his back and stomach. Like a bass with a fisherman's bait, it darted across the water's surface. Its head rose above the water as though intentionally displaying Kal's kicking legs. Shaking its head like a canine, it tore through the spinal column and musculature. Kal's severed back half fell free. They sank below the waves, soon to be lunch for other critters in the ocean.

Aboard the *Ritualist*, Arthur scrambled for the customized AR-15 he had on the flying bridge. Everyone knew he had illegally altered it to shoot at full auto. Now, they expected to see it in action.

With shaky hands, he tried loading the weapon. He cursed and stomped on the deck, failing to get the magazine in. Unknown to those observing from the other vessels, he was trying to load the thing backwards. It took a minute for him to recognize the problem and correct it.

He pointed the gun at the shape in the water. The fish was closing in like a torpedo at alarming speed, its head three meters from the bow.

Two…

One…

Arthur squeezed the trigger and screamed for his life.

CRASH!

The boat shook from the intense impact. Its captain lost his footing, his aim whipping to the left, finger still squeezing the trigger.

Bullets zipped across the water. Most of them landed harmlessly in the ocean. A couple struck the transom of the *Gold Star.*

And one ended up in the belly of Captain Lon Burnham.

He collapsed to his knees, holding his stomach. His crewmates hurried up to him, shouting his name.

"Sweet Jesus!" Moody exclaimed. "Paul! We need to help him!"

"Get the first aid kit," Paul replied.

From afar, he heard a bloodcurdling cry. His eyes went to the *Ritualist*. It was covered in a wet, green substance. A giant grey cloud billowed from its bridge and forward section. Through the fog, he identified Arthur Faraday's silhouette. He was spinning around like a top, his hands clutching his face.

Little by little, pieces of that silhouette peeled away, until there was literally a skeleton slumped over the side of the bridge.

At the same time, the front of the *Ritualist* was dissolving, revealing its inner components. Water rushed inside, adding enough weight to the vessel to pull it to the depths.

The sight was horrible, but mesmerizing, making Paul oblivious to the cigar-shaped creature making a run at the *Gold Star*. Its two crewmen, who were busy acting as paramedics for Lon Burnham, also did not notice its approach—not until it breached the water and slammed its mass on their transom.

The bow of the *Ritualist* shifted upward, tossing the two crewmen off of its flying bridge.

Freddy's feet hit the ladder as he fell backwards, flipping him upside down. He came down headfirst on the aft deck, breaking his neck on impact.

Landing near his twitching body was Taggert. He landed on his back. In the moments that followed, he realized he was sliding down a thirty-degree slope. At its bottom were the jaws of a horrifically deformed shark.

Huge jaws stretched open over the broken transom, spewing slime from its gums.

Taggert clawed at the deck in hopes of stopping his descent.

"Oh, God! Help me!!!"

He slid right into that open mouth.

The fish did not bother slipping back into the water. It was content with munching its victim right there on the spot. Blood mixed with slime, spewing from both the shark's mouth and gills.

Taggert's body clung to life, and by the way those legs were kicking outside the shark's mouth, it was an agonizing final minute.

All the while, water rushed onto the deck and spilled through the cracks that had formed under the shark's weight. Slowly, the stern lowered farther into the water.

Eventually, the slope was steep enough for the shark to slip free. Its basic shape was visible under the surface, enabling the last remaining trio of hunters to track its movements.

Moody was crippled by shock. His hands were clasped behind his head while he watched the bow of the *Gold Star* slowly rise. Its captain had succumbed to his bullet wound and was flopping down the vessel's decks.

"Snap out of it!" Paul said.

He swung the vessel in a sharp U-turn, facing the bow to the fish. Behind him, Harold was getting ready to drop the nets.

Paul grabbed his shotgun and pointed its double-barrel to the water. The shark was coming in fast. With each passing moment, it increased speed.

"Lower the nets!" he shouted to Harold.

The nets hit the water and dropped beneath the keel.

Up ahead, the shark came within ten feet.

Paul fired both barrels at its snout. Several tiny splashes preceded the pellets' impact against their target. Paul had timed the shot perfectly, the hit causing the fish to pass underneath the boat as opposed to ramming it.

The lines went taut.

Harold whooped. The fish was caught in the net.

His celebration was short-lived. The bow rose a few degrees, the outriggers shifting back a few inches.

The *Great Barrier Chief* started moving backwards.

Paul looked beyond the transom. He tried to convince himself that what he was looking at was a figment of his imagination. But it was not. The shark was actually pulling them backward.

He put the boat in full throttle.

A stalemate of opposing forces ensued, neither boat nor shark moving an inch, despite their best efforts.

"Shoot it!" he shouted to his crew. "Kill it! Hurry!"

Harold pumped his shotgun and unleashed a volley of pellets at the creature. Empty shells ejected from the port and hit the deck.

Moody was crouched by his black case. He opened it and pulled out a roll of dynamite. He broke the fuse, leaving only an inch-and-a-half.

A green cloud bloomed under the water. The ocean where the shark was thrashing suddenly began to sizzle.

"Its burning through the net!" Harold said. "What the hell is this freaking thing?"

Moody ran to the transom. He lit the end of the fuse with his cigarette lighter, brought it back over his shoulder, and let it fly.

The tension was lost. The lines went slack and the boat suddenly began flying forward.

Paul fell against the helm. He slowed the boat and looked at the water behind the boat. The water sizzled where their tug of war took place, emitting white steam into the air.

BOOM!

A tower of water reached to the sky while a titanic shockwave traveled beneath the vessel.

Paul brought the vessel to a stop and witnessed the aftermath.

Steam and mist scattered from the epicenter of the blast. The water rolled in large waves which gradually deteriorated as they spread farther out.

There was nothing on the fish-finder, nor was there any movement they could detect with the naked eye.

"What in the hell was that thing?" Paul said. Sweat rolled down his face. This was no ordinary shark. "The sheriff said it was fucked up because of some chemical shit that was dumped in the ocean. He didn't say anything about this being some sort of freak that shoots acid!"

"The better question is 'Where the hell is that thing?'" Harold said. "I don't see it anywhere. You think it's dead?"

Moody was standing near his case of dynamite, preparing another roll to be used in case the thing returned.

"I have no idea," he said. "I hope it's dead. Maybe we scared it off. But, honestly, I don't care enough to find out. I just want to get the hell out of here."

"No argument from me!" Harold replied. "To hell with the money. I wanna be back on land!"

Paul reloaded his shotgun. "I think we are in agreement, gentlemen." He turned the boat east and began driving it to that thin brownish line on the horizon that was the coast.

A few times through the recent years, he had received a few cash offers on his fishing vessel. He always turned them down, partly because of the low price, but mainly because fishing was the only thing he ever knew. After what he had just been through, however, he doubted he would ever want to go out on the water ever again. Not if monsters like that thing existed.

Nope, I'm gonna move inland, where the largest body of water is a rain puddle. I'll sell the boat, hopefully clear fifty grand after taxes, and figure out a new line of work. Beats getting eaten!

"Look at that!" Harold shouted. He pointed fifteen degrees starboard off the stern.

Paul took a glance. All he saw was ocean. Frankly, that was all he cared to see.

"There's nothing there!" he said.

"I swear I saw it," Harold said.

Moody joined him at the starboard quarter and looked to sea. "I don't see anything."

Harold snarled with impatience and stress. "Look, I'm telling you! It's coming after us. You think I would lie? Considering…" He gestured to the smoking remains of the *Ritualist*.

Moody watched the water again, still seeing nothing there.

Right then, the radio blared in the captain's ear. It was Sheriff Gillis' unpleasant voice.

"Paul? How's the fishing trip going?"

He snatched up the mic. "Terrible, Gillis! You didn't tell us…" He paused, not wanting to give too much away on an open channel. "You did not give us the full picture of what we were up against."

In the few moments of silence that followed that statement, he envisioned Gillis putting together the hidden meaning of what he was saying.

"Where's Burnham and Faraday?"

"Let's put it this way—they're out of commission."

"What?"

"That's right. That fish is not like anything God has put in these waters. I hope that client of yours saved a lot of cash doing you-know-what, because it has wrecked our livelihoods."

"Are you able to handle the issue?"

Paul blew an exasperated sigh. "Honestly, Sheriff, we don't know. We used dynamite on it, and the fish disappeared."

"Disappeared?"

"I have no idea where it is. We're getting out of dodge in case it shows up again."

"No, man," Harold called up to him. "I'm telling you, it's following us."

Paul ignored him. "If you want us to come back out here, there's gonna have to be some special conditions."

"Like what?"

"We're gonna need, let's just say, better equipment to get the job done. Oh, and triple the pay."

"Fine. Understood. The client agrees. For now, there's another issue at play. We're taking off from main harbor. I'd like you to link up with us. We need some extra hands in case things go south."

Paul digested those words. He knew Gillis had an eye on that EPA agent and Mark Wall's girlfriend. The only reason he would be so vague was because he planned to go through with putting an end to the investigation. To do that, they would have to box the agent's boat in and prevent his escape.

"What's in it for us?"

"Twenty grand for each of you."

Moody heard that. "Whoa! Okay, I can live with that."

"You do realize what he's asking, right?" Paul said to him.

Even Harold's demeanor changed. "Um, yeah. And that's fine with me. That agent guy's a nosey son of a bitch, anyway."

It was a good enough answer for Paul.

"Alright, Sheriff. We're on our way."

He placed the mic down and turned south to intercept Gillis.

Meanwhile, Harold continued watching the water. Not even the promise of twenty grand in his pocket eliminated his paranoia of the mutant shark following them.

CHAPTER 21

Julian moved the ice pack from his face to his ribs. In the hour since his brawl with Glenn, the aching had settled in. His ribs felt as though they were bent into his stomach and his chin had started swelling.

He spat into a wadded paper towel. His gums were still bleeding from a cracked crown he sustained from one of Glenn's haymakers.

"Damn, I'm gonna feel this for a while."

Maggie wrapped a towel over some ice from their cooler and brought it over to him. "I imagine the EPA has good dental insurance."

"They do, and thank God." Julian accepted the icepack from her and pressed it to his jaw. He checked the map he had purchased. On it was a red X he had drawn in place of the Darling Ravine.

"We're just about there."

He looked at the open sea and began experiencing his self-doubts. It was not as though there were mile markers or road signs directing him to the exact location. He had to use any landmarks available, many of which were underwater, to find his way.

A mile back, they passed the location of a shipwreck, which was marked by a yellow buoy. According to the map, the ridge was barely more than a mile southwest of that location.

"There!" Maggie pointed fifteen degrees off their port bow.

Julian squinted. Initially, he saw nothing but water. In the light of the sun was a tiny yellow speck.

"I see it." He turned the boat and moved closer to the thing. Sure enough, it was a buoy marker. It made sense; Mark may have known these fishing grounds well, but the ridge was narrow and required him to be in a precise location in order to dispose of the hazardous material.

He stopped the boat a few yards from the floating piece of plastic. "Time to put good ol' Jerico to use."

Maggie walked with him to the stern. Together, they lifted the orange and black drone over the side and lowered it to the water.

Julian performed a standard check of its rotors, ballast, and cameras. The machine was fully charged and ready to go.

His computer was switched on and placed under an umbrella for protection from the sun. If he were watched from afar, he would appear as nothing more than some guy enjoying some shade on his boat. Julian wished that was the reality. Nothing sounded better than enjoying some sunshine on the deck of a boat with a Mai Tai in his hand, particularly with Maggie accompanying him.

He was still buzzing from the progression of their partnership. The dopamine hit from their kiss had him sky high, and was probably helping to block some of the pain from his fight with Glenn.

The computer screen turned a greenish-blue as the drone initiated its descent. The depth in this region was four hundred and thirty feet, well within the drone's range.

As it neared eighty feet of depth, the screen began to darken.

Julian switched to the machine's underside camera. On the screen was a vast background comprised of light grey silt covering thick crust. In the middle of that undersea landscape was a long gorge. It was fairly narrow, only measuring around thirty feet at its widest point.

On each side of that gorge were several 'dots' of varying shapes and colors.

"What are those things?" Maggie asked.

Julian bit his tongue to keep from answering. He did not want to acknowledge the truth of what he was looking at. But as the drone went past two hundred feet, there was no denying what was covering the ocean floor.

It was an undersea graveyard. All life, flora and fauna, lay dead and decaying around a huge crack in the sea bottom.

Everywhere he looked, he saw sharks, cephalopods, bony fish, dolphins, all exposed to the leaking pollutants which turned the beautiful Gulf into a dead zone.

Maggie watched in stunned silence.

The casualties were not limited to the immediate area. Julian panned the fore and aft cameras to get a wider angle. As far as the eye could see was death. Seaweeds had changed from their natural green color to a light brown. All around them were crustaceans that used them for food and shelter. No animals, not even the intelligent octopuses that rotted in the middle of this graveyard, understood the danger they had been in. Animals that had burrows in the seafloor were equally unsafe as those swimming in the open. As soon as they pumped the toxic water through their gills, they were doomed.

To them, it was an invisible enemy. But to the trained eye, the source stuck out like a sore thumb, as such a thing was never meant to exist in such a beautiful environment.

Contrasting with the light grey seabed were numerous black metal drums.

Julian made sure his computer recorded the footage. He had found the dumping grounds, and it was far worse than he imagined.

The drums were everywhere. In their proper storage location, they were perfectly designed to contain their contents. A four-hundred-plus-foot drop in saltwater was more than enough to breach those barriers and contaminate the area. Curious fish and crustaceans had moved in on each one, believing to have found an easy meal.

Even worse, sharks and dolphins helped themselves to the infected fish, unaware of the poison in their system. It was a food chain of death.

Julian steered the drone to the gorge. He ignited a spotlight to provide a better view of the inside. As he predicted, many more drums were piled inside. There were dozens of them. Maybe even a hundred, all marked with warning labels.

"I can't believe Mark was doing this," Maggie said.

Julian felt his blood pressure spike. Why, in this day and age, would any entity, individual or corporation, think they could get away with this? They were in the 21st century now. Everyone knew about the dangers of improper disposal of hazardous materials. Human history was marred with terrible consequences of chemical spills.

There was the 1984 Bhopal disaster in India, in which a gas leak had killed thousands of civilians. In 2010, there was the Deepwater Horizon oil spill, the Baia Mare cyanide spill in Romania, the 1976 dioxin cloud in Seveso, Italy, and the Minamata disaster in Japan where many people suffered horrible effects from food contaminated with methylmercury.

At worst, many of those incidents were from terrible negligence. What Julian and Maggie were looking at was far worse. Goliath Industries intentionally dumped their waste in the ocean, fully aware of the environmental damage, all to save a few dollars.

Julian stepped away from the computer. "I've seen enough. Time to give my office a call."

"I'll get on the radio and get the Coast Guard out here," Maggie said. She moved to the flying bridge while Julian pulled out his smartphone. He attempted to get a call out, but got the three *beeps* of a phone with no signal.

"Damn."

"Julian?"

"Need me to speak to them?" he asked.

"No. Someone's coming."

Julian turned around and looked stern of the vessel. Three boats were on approach. Right away, he recognized two of them. The one leading the group was Sheriff Gillis' patrol boat. He had three deputies aboard his vessel, all of whom were armed with what appeared to be M1 Carbines.

Behind them was the *Lineman*, helmed by none other than Mark Wall. Standing on the flying bridge with him was Ria Thorne. Her hair was waving in the wind. Standing next to Maggie's ex-boyfriend, she made sure to wear an outfit that revealed plenty of cleavage. After all, she controlled Mark with more than just the promise of cash.

Julian needed to use binoculars to identify the third boat. Unlike the other two vessels, which were coming in from the east, it was coming from the north. When it came within seven hundred feet, he was able to make out the words on its bow.

Great Barrier Chief.

Julian had seen the boat at Pelican Grove's main harbor. During his time in the wacky town, he had seen most of the local fishermen and their vessels at some point. Most of them blended together in his memory, but a few stood out. One of those was the *Great Barrier Chief* and its three-man-crew, Paul Relan, Moody Ernst, and Harold Newsom.

They were the first bunch he ever had an altercation with. It was the day after he arrived in town when he saw them illegally finning some blue sharks. He had taken them to the local jail and had hoped Sheriff Gillis would help arrange a trial date. That day, Julian got his first glance of Gillis' true colors.

In a sense, watching this group of criminals made him want to laugh. There was a touch of irony in the way Goliath Industries was handling their situation. With so many people paid off to either dump the material or turn the other cheek, they were probably spending close to the amount needed to dispose of the stuff properly.

He kept his binoculars on the fishing vessel. One of the crewmen, Harold, was obsessively monitoring the water behind the boat. He was a nervous man searching for something.

As for everyone else, their eyes were on Julian and Maggie. The sheriff and the *Lineman* were coming directly at the agent. The *Great Barrier Chief* was hooking to the west, gradually turning to port in a path that would bring it in front of Julian's vessel.

"We're in trouble," he muttered.

"What do we do?" Maggie said.

Julian started the engine. "Run."

He put the boat into full throttle.

In direct response, the small band of vessels increased their speed to the max. The police cruiser proved to be the fastest by far, out-performing its companion vessels as well as the cruiser it was chasing.

Gillis' voice appeared over the radio.

"I'm gonna give you one chance to make this easy. Stop your boat and put your hands above your head. And toss your weapon overboard... yeah, I know you're armed."

Julian snatched the speaker mic. "So, Sheriff? What's the going rate for souls these days? How long have you been letting Goliath Industries foul up this entire area?"

"I truly admire your devotion, Agent. The rookie in you can be seen plain as day. Nobody cares about this town. Not even the people who live in it. It's been run into the ground by politicians who talk a big game, but accomplish nothing except milk the place for all it's worth, then move on to bigger and better things."

"Was that your goal? Become mayor of Pelican Grove? Bag a couple hundred grand, then retire?"

"The thought crossed my mind over the years. Suffice to say, I found a better way of solving that problem. Like I said, nobody cares about this place. So, why should I be bothered if some company dumps some useless shit in their fishing grounds?"

"I think you know the answer to that," Julian said.

He peeked over his shoulder. The Sheriff's cruiser was inching closer and closer. His own boat was moving at twenty knots. Gillis' was pushing at least twenty-five.

"There's more to it than the town," he continued. "This sludge can affect the waters off the entire panhandle. The effects on the environment are catastrophic at best. People swim in these waters, Sheriff. You're tainting a large portion of the food supply. And there's more: I have evidence to show exposure to the cocktail of toxins down in the ravine acts as a horrible mutagen. You're not just dirtying the waters, Sheriff. You're creating literal sea monsters."

"Yeah, keep monologuing, Agent."

There was no sense of doubt or disbelief in the Sheriff's voice. Anyone else would have mocked him for making such a claim, especially someone who was trying to justify and cover-up the pollution.

"You know what I'm talking about, don't you?"

"The problem was handled this morning. I'd say you have nothing to worry about, but then I'd be lying."

"Sheriff, quit toying with him and get this over with!"

"That's Ria Thorne," Maggie said to Julian.

"It'll be done shortly," the sheriff assured his client. His next statement was directed at Julian. *"The shark was an anomaly. A one in a million. Everything else that comes into contact with our barrels dies. So, if you're going to make a statement of how we endanger human life,*

you can stick it up your ass and get with the program. Now, stop your boat. My client was considering making a deal with you. It's the easiest, cleanest way to solve our differences. Otherwise, we'll have to resort to something a little messier—for you AND your girlfriend."

Maggie snatched the mic. "Stick that cash up your fat ass, Sheriff." She handed it back to the agent.

"My sentiments exactly. Oh, and by the way, the shark was *not* an anomaly. We encountered one last night. A twelve-footer with a violent disposition and a tendency to spray acid at anything it didn't like. And these mutants will attack anything they see. They exist in excruciating pain, and as a result, they are extremely aggressive."

The next several moments went by with radio silence.

Gillis was starting to come up on their port side. The deputies gathered at the gunwale with rifles aimed.

With outrunning them out of the question, Julian decided to go for something more drastic.

He whipped the cruiser to port, sideswiping the Sheriff's boat. The men on deck stumbled from their firing positions as the entire boat juddered. Julian kept up the pressure, skating by the bow of the police boat until he was heading east.

Sheriff Gillis sent a few shots in his direction.

"Paul! Get closer."

Julian looked to the northeast. "Shit!"

While he was distracted on outrunning the Sheriff, the *Great Barrier Chief* backtracked to the east, knowing that Julian would eventually attempt to make a go for dry land.

The sixty-foot trawler was directly ahead of him, its bow facing south. On its main deck was Moody. He held a roll of dynamite in his hand. Even in the bright sunlight, the sparking of its fuse could not be missed.

"Oh, my God! Julian!" Maggie cried.

He veered farther to port, passing the trawler.

Moody tossed the dynamite in their direction. It touched the water within twelve feet of their vessel. At that very moment, it detonated.

Julian and Maggie were struck by a seemingly invisible force. The stern lifted and fell. Water surged over the sides onto the deck. A large wave of water rolled and crested, carrying the boat with it for several meters.

He fell to his knees and used his body to cover Maggie's. He heard the motor clank and grind before stalling altogether.

The three boats formed a perimeter around the disabled cruiser, boxing it in.

Sheriff Gillis placed his radio mic down and resorted to shouting directly at those crouched near the helm. “Your luck’s run out, Reed.”

Julian stood up, hand on his pistol. He made sure to look the sheriff dead in the eye.

“And how exactly are you going to explain this to the EPA? Last I checked, they aren’t particularly fond of having their agents executed.”

Gillis laughed. “Easy. You see, you took your boat out to sea to hunt a killer shark that was giving our community some grief. In the process, you were brutally killed by the shark and lost to sea. No body. At least you’ll get some bagpipes and American flags at your funeral.” He tilted his head in thought. “Wait… do they do that for the Environmental Protection Agency?”

He looked at his deputies, all of whom shrugged.

“I guess there’s only one way to find out.”

“Yeah?” Julian snapped. He pointed his thumb at the stern of his boat. The transom and prop had been blown out by the dynamite explosion, immobilizing them. “And how are you going to explain this? They’re obviously not going to think a shark did that.”

“Easy,” Mark shouted. “You guys illegally got ahold of some dynamite and tried to use it on the shark. But because you were so inept, you ended up blowing yourselves up instead. Simple as that.”

Maggie stood up so she could look the piece of shit in the eye.

“You’re a real piece of shit, you know that?”

Mark smiled proudly and put his arms out. “Hey, you were once all over this piece of shit. And you loved every moment of it, baby! You could’ve stayed. We could’ve easily worked things out. But that temper of yours has a way of getting in the way of smart thinking. That’s why you lost your job, it’s why you’ve never amounted to anything, it’s why you’re broke—it’s why you’re on that asshole’s boat instead of mine right now.”

Maggie took Julian’s hand. “I’d rather sink to the bottom of the ocean with him than live one more second with you.”

Mark snorted. “How romantic.”

Ria winked. “More for me.” She rubbed her hand over Mark’s jaw as she spoke, watching his ex-girlfriend in hopes of getting an angry response.

There was nothing for Maggie to be offended over. If anything, she felt like she had wasted too many years with that piece of dirt.

“You two deserve each other. You’re practically two turds circling the drain.”

Ria dropped her hand in offense to that statement; a gesture that gave Maggie immense satisfaction. Since their first meeting, she suspected the company rep was a princess in her own mind.

"And by the way, you ought to clean the inside of your car," she continued. "And I'd learn to lock your phone if I was you. You never know what sensitive information someone might learn."

Ria gave her the finger, then looked over at the men aboard the *Great Barrier Chief.*

"Blow them to hell."

Moody was on the deck with a roll of dynamite in one hand and his lighter in the other.

"These days, there are so many complex explosives out there. But there's something about old-fashioned dynamite that, I don't know, brings a smile to my face. It makes me feel like I live in the Old West."

"Less talking and more blowing!" Harold said.

Moody looked at him with one eyebrow raised.

Harold groaned and broke eye contact. "Yes, that did not come out quite right."

"That's putting it mildly." Chuckling, he started flicking his lighter. "Sheriff? You gonna, you know, pew-pew them first?"

"Only if he goes for that piece of junk at his hip," Gillis said. "But he knows he's not a fast draw. And there are a bunch of guns on him already."

"I want them alive to experience this," Ria said with a childlike giddiness. "I want to see if I can actually see their bodies break apart in real time."

Julian exhaled. He gave thought to popping a round through the company rep before being overwhelmed by enemy gunfire and explosives. Looking at those deputies, he knew he had no chance.

Instead, he focused on the touch of Maggie's hand. There was greater peace and comfort in this basic human connection than he would ever get from a violent act of retaliation.

Her hand squeezed his. Maggie was thinking the same thing.

"Thanks for saving me," she said.

"But I didn't," he replied.

"No, you did. I was wasting my life up until now. I'd rather go out with some dignity than begging for scraps on the street."

Julian did not say anything. Maggie was at peace with their circumstance. He chose to let her die with it, just as he intended to.

Mark lit the fuse and looked at his victims.

"Think of it this way: at least you're going out with a bang!" He joined the others in sadistic laughter as he reared his hand back to throw the explosive.

***

Its entire existence was one of pain. Unknown to its simple mind, the large fish endured the endless firing of nerve signals. From the tip of its snout to the lobes of its massive caudal fin, it was in agony. Swelling in various areas of its musculature pushed on its nerves. In other areas, its musculature system and cartilage skeleton were not properly formed, resulting in benign growths. To the fish, it felt as though it was constantly being impaled by a massive tooth.

There was no getting used to the pain. In the shark's mind, it was constantly under attack. The only change was the manner in which the pain was registered. At times, it was a static, constant ache. Other times, sharp pulses, like stabbing motions, rippled from the knots in its skeleton.

Today, there was new pain. The scent of its own blood confirmed that the land-based organisms aboard those moving floating structures had harmed it. After the burst of sound and energy following its escape from the mesh, the fish slowed its speed to allow a moment to recover.

All the while, it kept track of that third vessel. It went north for five miles, eventually linking up with three other machines. They were huddled in a group, similarly how some species of bony fish kept in close proximity to one another.

The largest of the bunch was the one that had nearly snagged it in the mesh object. Soundwaves from the creatures standing atop of it reached the shark. Recognizing them as the same voices it detected during their recent clash, the shark instinctively moved in on their vessel.

It increased its speed, extended its jaws, and ascended at the vessel, ready to finish the fight.

***

Moody started bringing his arm forward.

His throw was cut short by a wall of water cresting over the starboard quarter. In that water were gelatinous strands of slime.

Then came the pointed snout of a large toxic shark. It brought its neck onto the vessel and shut its jaws over the fisherman. Huge teeth punctured Moody, who was dragged screaming off of the boat.

Paul and Harold burst into hysterics, initially from the sudden appearance of the shark and the taking of Moody, and then from the sight of the burning fuse on their deck.

Paul took cover and tucked his head low.

Harold ran for the bundle of dynamite. He picked it up with hopes of tossing it overboard. He lived just long enough to see the last few millimeters of fuse burn away.

"Sh—"

BANG!

Pieces of boat and Harold flew in all directions. The *Great Barrier Chief* rocked forward, then aft. From there, it momentarily settled on a twenty-degree angle. Over the next several seconds, the stern plunged deeper into the Gulf.

Paul looked down at the water as his boat slipped beneath its surface. Within that water were strands of that vile slimy substance.

"Oh, dear God, no. Please, don't let me die like this."

The shark raised its head above the water.

Lying across its jaws was Moody Ernst, his head and feet dangling outside the corners of its mouth. Everything between resembled ground beef in the shark's mouth. He was looking to his captain, spitting blood while muttering, "H-help me!"

A final chomp of those jaws cut through the spinal column and shinbones, dropping his head and feet into the ocean.

Paul grabbed his double-barrel shotgun and put his feet against the top ladder bar, propping himself on the flying bridge while he took aim.

The shark proved to be the faster draw.

A jet of burning-hot acid struck the fisherman right in the stomach. Gagging from a magnitude of pain he did not know was possible, Paul looked down at himself. With gasps of agony and shock, he watched his shirt and skin liquify, and his guts spill out of him.

His gun fell from his grasp and came down on two rail bars on the flying bridge. Paul fell on his back, dead.

The shark took no notice of his corpse falling from the bridge to the main deck, for its attention had shifted to the remaining boats.

Maggie clung to Julian. Two emotions put her mind in a merry-go-round. She was relieved to see the black-hearted fishermen get foiled in their attempt to kill her and Julian. At the same time, the sight of such a huge shark filled her heart with crippling fear.

Watching the speed in which the sheriff attempted an escape, she was not alone in the latter.

Sheriff Gillis put his boat in full-throttle and pulled away from their encirclement. The three deputies were scrambling on deck, unsure of what to do. The explosion had sent fragments of the trawler smashing against their boat, marking its already deteriorating paint job.

Mark Wall was also pulling away, exclaiming, "To hell with this!"

As a result, Ria Thorne began grabbing at him in protest. "What arc you doing? There's still work that needs to be done."

"Like I said," Mark replied to her. "To hell with this!"

The fish went after the moving targets.

Sheriff Gillis gave his men a scalding look. They resembled confused school children on their first day of class, unsure of what to do.

In the water beyond them was the huge dorsal fin.

"What the hell are you idiots waiting for?" he said. "Shoot the damn thing!"

The deputies assembled at the rear and took aim. Gunshots cracked the air, delivering deadly projectiles at the beast. Red clouds took form in the shark's wake.

It did not slow down. On the contrary, it appeared to gain speed.

A spout of bloody water burst, preceding the appearance of the shark's nasty face.

The deputies shot at it some more, blowing fleshy holes in its snout and chin. One of the bullets punched through one of its teeth before burrowing in the back of its throat.

Gillis took another look. The pore on the creature's snout was pulsing. Having witnessed Paul Relan's fate, he knew exactly what was in store for him.

Cursing, he veered sharply to port.

The sudden turn caught his deputies by surprise. One of them, who stood at the starboard corner of the transom, flipped in an involuntary cartwheel motion overboard.

A spray of acid streaked across the air where the boat had been a moment prior.

Gillis watched the sizzling sea behind him, keeping the boat hooking leftward. A pang of superiority lifted his spirits. He had outsmarted the dumb fish.

"Sheriff! What the fuck!"

Gillis turned his eyes forward. In front of him was the *Great Barrier Chief*, moving straight across his path.

"SHIT! SHIT! SHIT!"

Gillis turned the wheel to starboard.

His portside smacked against the trawler's bow, shuddering the police boat. It skidded northwards, clearing the larger vessel. The engine stalled, leaving the corrupt law enforcement officers adrift.

Gillis felt uncontrollable shakes in his hands as he hurriedly attempted to restart the engine.

"AGH!"

Out in the water was the shark's head thrashing back and forth like a dog. Impaled by its teeth was the deputy who had fallen overboard. He reached out with his one good hand, pleading for help.

The shark completed its bite.

The man dropped into the water, with a half circle bitemark running down his left armpit down to his pelvis, where his leg barely remained attached by a few strands of meat.

"It's coming," one of the deputies cried.

Indeed, it was, and at cheetah speed.

The men began discharging their rifles, pulling off a few shots before the beast launched itself out of the water. Traveling in a perfect arch, it came down head-first on the vessel.

One of the deputies ended up right under the shark's belly. Pinned to the deck, his body popped like a grape, reducing him to a red soupy mixture.

The shark corkscrewed, burrowing its head through the damaged deck, effectively splitting the boat in half.

Its tail swung like a tennis racket, smacking the last remaining deputy right off the boat. He flew across the air like a birdie in a game of badminton, bending in ways that were only possible for a man with a decimated skeleton.

The stern of the police boat broke away entirely.

Gillis clung to the helm as the forward half tilted upright. Below his feet were the shark's greenish-yellow teeth. Strands of fabric dangled from their serrated edges. Nauseating waste spewed from its gills and the back of its throat.

He bent his knees and pulled his feet up. The huge black snout lifted another eighteen inches, revealing its many small pores, and its large deadly one.

Growling, the sheriff unholstered his pistol.

"Die, you bitch!"

He put several rounds into the shark's head.

It did not flee. Absorbing the punishment, the shark waited for the bow to finish sinking.

Gillis whimpered. He was sinking, not into water, but right into the shark's mouth. He looked at his pistol, regretting having used up his entire magazine on the shark instead of saving the last bullet for himself.

"No… NOOOOO!!!"

The fish stretched its mouth open and took the sheriff's entire body. Gillis scrambled in its throat, having bypassed its teeth straight for a free pass into its gullet.

There, he was subject to a different kind of acid. As opposed to that which the fish ejected through its pores, this particular acid bath took a little more time.

The fish swam off for its next target, unbothered by the sound of screams echoing from inside its stomach.

"Damn it, Mark! Turn the boat around!"

Mark Wall thrust his hand to the side to fend off the maniac business rep. What he once found to be sexy qualities were now a hindrance to the basic desire to survive.

She pulled at his arm and pointed a finger to the dumping ground. "You still have several barrels here. We need to get rid of them!"

A dumbfounded Mark looked over at her. "Are you insane? Did you not just witness what happened back there?"

"Yes!" she exclaimed. "And it's nothing compared to what'll happen to me if we don't complete the assignment! And we can't leave those witnesses alive. If they haven't already notified somebody, they will when they get back to shore."

Mark replied with spit-spewing laughter.

"That's *your* problem, girl."

"Yours too!"

"Not a snowball's chance in hell." Mark pushed her away after she attempted to grab the helm. Ria stumbled back against the railing and gave a glance at the shoreline on the horizon. Mark, driving with one hand, warned her with a raised finger and a very stern tone of voice. "I'm not dying on account of you, bitch. You want that stuff dumped? I guess you'll just have to do it yourself."

Ria's face tensed. She inhaled through her nose, winding up for her response.

Mark anticipated an endless filibuster or, at worst, another attempt to take control of the helm.

What he got was much worse.

She pulled up the back of her shirt and pulled out a small snub-nose revolver.

An ice-cold shiver ran down Mark's spine. He released the wheel and backed to the other side of the flying bridge. He had spent weeks with this woman. He had stripped her clothes off her body and enjoyed the physical pleasures she had to offer. Not once did he see a gun in her wardrobe.

That left one conclusion: she deliberately kept it secret so when it came time to use it on an unruly contractor or competitor, they would be caught off guard. Just like Mark was feeling now.

He put a hand out. “Now wait…”

Bang!

Mark grabbed his abdomen, feeling warm blood pouring between his fingers. A fierce pain dropped him to his knees. He gasped for breath, feeling his insides enflaming.

Ria tucked the revolver in her jeans and took control of the helm. She turned the boat around and made her way back to the drop-off area.

The shark was nowhere to be seen. Sheriff Gillis and his deputies were dead, the agent and Mark’s ex were stranded, and the *Great Barrier Chief* was half-submerged with its bow at a forty-five-degree angle.

Mark, holding his insides in with one hand, scooted to the instrument panel. Ria kicked him in the jaw, rolling him backward.

He dry-heaved and squirmed in place, his insides feeling as though they were on fire.

“Help me!”

“I was helping you, you stupid moron,” Ria snapped. “You were a broke loser when I found you. That changed because of *me*. All you had to do was finish the job.”

“But… the shark!”

“How hard can it be to kill a goddamn fish?!” She looked at her snub nose revolver. Of its five-bullet capacity, four remained. “Two for the agent, two for the chick.”

“Help me!” Mark gasped a second time.

“Stop being such a baby,” Ria muttered.

“You shot me!”

“If I had more bullets, I’d do it again just to shut you up.”

Mark watched the blood pumping from his middle. Every motion was excruciating. Even breathing was pure torture.

Yet, there was one thing surpassing that pain.

Anger.

Like a feral beast, he planted his feet on the deck and threw himself at Ria. She spun to her left and extended her gun. Bloody hands grabbed her wrist and redirected the gun aft.

All four remaining rounds discharged right into the barrels on the main deck. A metallic chemical smell filled the air within seconds.

Ria fought to free the weapon. Mark, still losing blood through his abdominal wound, was quickly losing steam. Taking advantage of this,

Ria raised a knee into his groin. Dislodging her hand from his grasp, she whacked him in the temple with the revolver.

Mark fell on his right side. There, he remained while curling into a fetal position.

Ria turned her eyes forward, then screamed.

Directly in front of the boat was the shark. A thick, concentrated spray of acid spewed from its snout right at her face.

The stream moved over her shoulders, splattering all over the chemical shipment on the main deck behind her.

Mark watched his client and lover flapping her arms wildly, her head completely lost in the green current—literally.

The shark ceased its acid spray and dove, evading an impact from the vessel. Standing there at the helm was Ria Thorne. The blank eye sockets of a smoking skull gazed at the open ocean.

Her corpse tilted to the left, twisted, and fell…right on top of Mark. Those eye sockets were level with his own, the forehead smoking, the jaw nearly touching his lips as though her corpse was attempting to steal a kiss.

"Agh! Get off me!"

He shoved the dead company rep to the side and scrambled for the controls. Throttling back, he brought the boat to a stop.

The pain in his abdomen increased, and Mark leaned over the console. "Oh, God!"

A splash from the shark's reemergence made him reel backward. The fish struck the keel, shifting the *Lineman* and knocking over some of the barrels. A second impact put the weakened Mark Wall on his ass. The escalating turbulence pushed him backward to the ladder.

Rolling over his shoulder like a human wheel, he plummeted from the structure to the main deck.

Suddenly, he felt heat. *Lots* of heat. Burning heat.

Looking at himself, he saw the flames working their way across his body. He looked left and right at the spilled substance oozing from the barrels and the acid burns on the deck. The mixture of substances resulted in a hot fire that he now lay in the middle of.

He brushed his body with his hands, accomplishing nothing but spreading it further.

Pain and terror ravaged Mark's body and mind, sparing nothing except his soul.

A worse fire awaited that.

Julian looked away. There was no use in witnessing every moment of Mark's demise. The guy was a piece of shit who had nobody but himself to blame for his circumstances. In a sense, he was deserving of such a fate, especially when one considered the fact he was about to be an accessory to murder. Still, Julian and Maggie felt no joy in the anguish of his final moments. They were human after all.

Their focus shifted to their present reality. Their boat was disabled, as was its radio. All they had in their favor was Julian's pistol.

Fifteen yards south of their position was the shark's dorsal fin.

"Keep quiet," Julian whispered. "Don't cause any sudden movements. It probably doesn't even know we're here."

Maggie looked at her jittery hands. "Easier said than done."

They watched the mutated fish move at a leisurely pace to the half-submerged *Great Barrier Chief.* It bumped the wreckage with its snout in search of any stragglers.

Julian noticed movement on the flying bridge. He grabbed his pair of binoculars and got a magnified look at the source.

A double-barrel shotgun rested on the rail bars.

He lowered the glasses and grumbled at the twenty-five feet of distance between himself and the trawler.

"So close, yet so far."

"Yeah, good luck killing it with that thing anyway," Maggie whispered. "Unless you managed to get a shot to the brain, that shark will shrug off anything we throw its way. Unless, of course, you have a grenade launcher lying around somewhere."

"Left it in my other pants," he replied. He looked at his pistol and contemplated whether his idea would work with it. He came to the conclusion of, "I'll lose my damn arm in the process."

Maggie looked at the man beside her talking to himself. "Um, you okay there?"

"Hmm? I guess it depends on whether we get out of here alive," he said.

"In other words, you're *not* okay," she replied. "I don't see how we're ever getting away from here. What was your plan, anyway?"

Julian nudged his head in the shark's direction. "I know where that thing stores its acid supply. Its in the neck, above its right gill slits."

"And that's important, why?"

"If we can rupture it before the creature unloads its contents, we can literally melt the bastard from the inside out. It's not completely immune to its own supply."

Maggie began obsessively looking at his pistol. Now it made sense why he needed to get up close and personal. Bullets could hurt the fish, but its skin was thick, meaning they might not penetrate deep enough to damage the sack. But a shotgun blast through its gill would do the trick.

Part of her wanted to ask, 'Why not just shoot the thing through the roof of the mouth and obliterate its brain?' The answer came to her on its own; *because if you're in front of the shark, you're probably gonna be too busy getting chomped on.*

The first order of business was getting that shotgun.

The dorsal fin was heading north again, moving at a leisurely pace. It was not going away anytime soon. Even if rescue came, they would only be added to the body count. Almost everyone who knew of the shark's secret weapon was dead.

Maggie watched the water for anything that could serve as a distraction.

BOOM!

She and Julian juddered as one of the barrels aboard the *Lineman* exploded. The shark moved in the opposite direction, but quickly slowed down and resumed circling the vessels.

"Damn barrels," Julian grumbled. "They were gonna drop those into the ridge… right along with us."

The mention of the ridge triggered a surge in Maggie's mind. She looked down at the main deck at Julian's computer and control system.

"The drone! You can distract it with the drone long enough for one of us to swim over to that other boat."

Julian stood up. He could not believe he didn't think of that himself.

"Damn, you're right!"

Slowly, they lowered themselves to the main deck. The entire stern had been ravaged by the dynamite blast, leaving the transom and deck heavily deformed.

The computer appeared to be okay, minus a crack that stretched across its screen.

Julian brought up the camera feeds. It was still in the gorge where Mark had been dumping his barrels.

"Are you able to pilot it from this far out?"

It was a question that made Julian nervous. In their efforts to escape Gillis' posse, they had gone at least a half mile, which was the limit for their wireless controller.

"Only one way to find out."

He ordered the sub to ascend.

Right away, the machine elevated above the gorge. It was responding to his command.

Julian quietly pumped his fist. "Yes!"

He checked the GPS, gauging its position compared to theirs. To his surprise, they had not retreated as far as he had thought. Those zigzags during the chase caused him to move in a partial circle.

The drone approached at its maximum speed.

All the while, the shark continued circling. It gradually moved closer to their boat. Julian grew increasingly anxious. No amount of self-calming exercises could get his heart rate to slow down.

Maggie watched the north with her binoculars.

"There! I see it."

Julian followed her finger with his eyes. It took another minute of travel before it could be seen with the naked eye.

"There."

He steered the thing to the bits of floating debris that once belonged to Sheriff Gillis' boat. Using the drone's miniature drill, meant for collecting soil samples, he dug into one of the fragments.

The vibration was low, but audible enough to get the shark's attention.

He reversed the machine and led the shark farther out to sea.

"It's working," Maggie said.

Julian put the control in her hands. He then gave her the pistol.

"Don't shoot unless you have no other choice," he said.

"But Julian…"

He refused to drag this out. The agent threw himself into the water and went for the *Great Barrier Chief.*

Saltwater assaulted his eyes and forced its way down his throat, making him dry-heave. He paddled his arms in wide circles, his feet kicking fiercely.

In under a minute, he had closed within fifteen feet of the trawler.

"Julian! It's coming back!" Maggie shouted.

The agent did his best to quicken his pace. He was twelve feet away now.

"It's ignoring the drone! It's coming right to you!"

Damn it!

He had considered the possibility that the shark would have abandoned the drone in preference of going after prey with an actual heartbeat. Optimism bias on his part made him believe it would go after the drone because it was closer.

Julian suppressed a yell. He was within five feet.

So close! Almost there.

A surge of water hit him from behind. The force behind that small wave extended its jaws, ready to tear the agent to pieces.

Gunshots cracked the sky. The fish jerked to the left, bypassing Julian and turning around.

Julian rode the current the rest of the way to the *Great Barrier Chief.* He grabbed ahold of the railing on the gunnel and pulled himself up its slope.

He stopped midway up and looked at Maggie. She was crouched on their cruiser, her weapon pointed at the water.

"Nice shooting!" he called to her.

"Thanks. First time, honestly."

Julian whistled. "Never before have I been so grateful for beginner's luck." He moved up to the flying bridge. The shotgun was right there, waiting to be snatched. And snatch it, he did.

He breached the weapon to confirm it was loaded, then gave a thumbs up to Maggie.

"I lost track of it," she said.

"Leave that part to me," he responded.

He returned to what remained of the main deck, partially submerging himself in seawater. Securing himself with a line from the starboard outrigger, he held himself in place, while watching the sea.

The frustration was immediate. This was the one time he wanted the shark to appear, and yet, it was nowhere to be seen.

"Where the hell are you?"

Tucking the gun in his armpit, he grabbed a piece of loose decking and bashed it against the hull of the boat.

Dull sounds of impact reverberated through the water.

Again and again, he smacked the hull.

"Come on. Come get me."

Another hit sent a wave of vibration.

"You know I'm here. Come get me."

He smacked the hull again… and the cone-shaped head emerged.

The shark arose with a triumphant splash, jaws agape. Julian extended the shotgun toward its gills.

The fish, seeing the meat of his arms, whipped its head to the side. Julian was knocked against the deck. *Boom!* The first barrel went off, wasted on the sky.

"Shit!"

He had one barrel left. One chance to kill that fish.

There were bigger problems than how many shells he had left. Julian felt himself sliding down, right into the shark's mouth.

The fish identified a target and closed its jaws over his left leg.

Julian threw his head back and screamed in agony. A split-second later, his screams were drowned out by the sea. The fish had taken off running, dragging him with the corner of its mouth.

He could feel the tips of those horrible teeth digging into his shinbones. Water splashed his face and blurred his vision.

The shotgun was still in his hand. Julian refused to release his grip. Additionally, the muscle contractions resulting from the pain of muscle tissue and tendons being sliced.

He was dragged for twenty yards before the shark slowed. The jaws widened, releasing Julian.

When the agent popped up from underwater, he heard the shots from his pistol. Maggie was saving his ass for the second time in a row with her natural marksmanship. The fish was not having it this time.

Julian recognized the curve in its body. It was turning around with intent to melt her down to the bone.

He reached out with his free hand and grasped the edge of the shark's right pectoral fin.

Its tail fluttered, propelling the shark, and Julian, towards the cruiser.

A second rush of water threatened to pull the agent off of the fish. He dug his fingernails into the rough skin, spitting seawater from his mouth, all while barely maintaining a hold on the shotgun.

The creature slowed as it reached the cruiser.

Maggie fired her last shot, then tossed the empty weapon at its nose. The shark lifted its head and gazed at her with those ugly green eyes. The muscles on its neck began to pulse, prepping for a violent contraction that would expel its acid supply.

Julian had only a window of a few seconds. He climbed over the fin, then pushed off of it with his good foot, lining him right up beside the creature's neck.

The head shifted to the right, its eye catching a glimpse of the agent as he stuck the gun barrel through its middle gill slit.

"Feel the burn."

BANG!

The fish lurched, tossing the agent out of the water.

Julian landed on the other side of his cruiser. The sound of Maggie's voice cut his disorientation short. She turned to his left and made eye contact with him. A line with a small inflatable donut came his way.

He gladly grabbed ahold of it and rested while she pulled him closer.

She was in tears after seeing the state of his leg.

"Oh, my God, Julian. You're hurt bad."

"I'll live," he said. "More importantly, *you'll* live."

A cloud of smoke spewed from the center of a mass of raging water. The shark twisted itself into all sorts of positions, unable to undo the burning pain that was eating it from the inside out. It struck the burning wreckage of the *Lineman*, turned around, and barrel-rolled. There was no strategy to its actions; just instinctual responses to unimaginable pain.

It flipped upside down, revealing its pale underside.

Maggie hugged Julian close, watching in disgust as the shark's throat and stomach split wide open. Liquified guts spilled into the water like lava from a volcano, sizzling as they were rapidly cooled.

The motions ceased.

Void of life, the shark sank to the ocean floor, leaving a thick trail of blood and melted guts in its wake.

Maggie put her head on Julian's shoulder. It was done. The shark was dead, as were those responsible for its creation.

In the minutes that followed, she opened the first aid kit and tightly wrapped some bandages around Julian's injured leg. It was a temporary measure, but it would hold until he could get into a hospital.

"I might have to think twice before involving myself in any more E.P.A. investigations."

Julian smiled. "I wouldn't worry about that."

She looked him in the eye. "Right. You're going back to that town."

"I am," he said. "But, there's a little more to it. The chief is retiring and the deputy chief is taking his spot. They were thinking of making me the next deputy chief. In five or ten years, once the replacement chief retires, the town would elevate me to the top spot."

Maggie smiled. "Wow! I guess you really have good connections."

"I had a phone conversation with them," he said. "They said it was contingent on my performance with the EPA. I think it was the chief's way of making me earn the job."

Maggie looked at the computer. In its hard drive was a myriad of evidence.

"I think you did."

"I'd like to think so." He squeezed her hand. "Thanks to your help."

She lowered her head. "I guess that means you'll be leaving soon."

Julian nodded.

"You know, uh, there's a place in town… a local diner. It's nothing much—maybe fifteen tables. But it's a nice little place."

Maggie started reading between the lines. "Yeah?"

"The lady who runs it is really sweet. Very kind-hearted. She was hoping to pass the business on to her kids, but they moved far away in pursuit of other interests. She said she would only sell the place to someone who she knew would take good care of it."

Maggie had a hand on his shoulder. "You think I should—"

"Absolutely."

She smiled. "But… how could I buy it? I don't have money, and I would never qualify for a loan."

"On your own, maybe not. But with a co-signer, things might work out." Julian cleared his throat. "And that co-signer might know a place where you can stay."

Maggie could not hold off any longer. She pulled Julian close and pressed her lips to his.

On this nightmare of a day, she felt happier and more alive than ever.

The End

Check out other great

Sea Monster Novels!

C.J. Waller

PREDATOR X

When deep level oil fracking uncovers a vast subterranean sea, a crack team of cavers and scientists are sent down to investigate. Upon their arrival, they disappear without a trace. A second team, including sedimentologist Dr Megan Stoker, are ordered to seek out Alpha Team and report back their findings. But Alpha team are nowhere to be found – instead, they are faced with something unexpected in the depths. Something ancient. Something huge. Something dangerous. Predator X

Robert J. Stava

NEPTUNES RECKONING

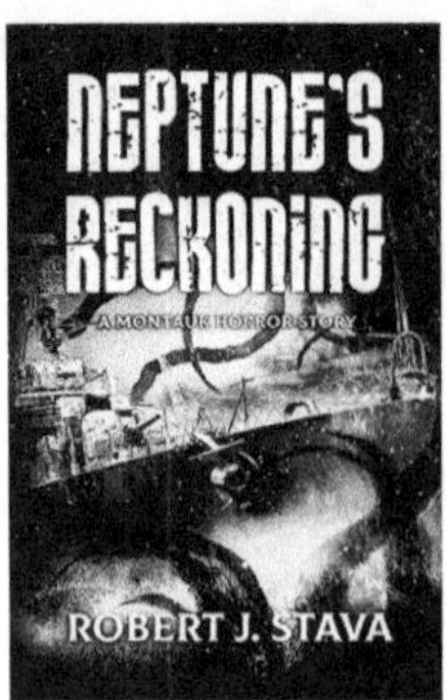

At the easternmost end of Long Island lies a seaside town known as Montauk. Ground Zero on the Eastern seaboard for all manner of conspiracy theories involving it's hidden Cold War military base, rumors of time-travel experiments and alien visitors... For renowned Naval historian William Vanek it's the where his grandfather's ship went down on a Top Secret mission during WWII code-named "Neptune's Reckoning". Together with Marine Biologist Daniel Cheung and disgraced French underwater explorer Arnaud Navarre, he's about to discover the truth behind the urban legends: a nightmare from beyond space and time that has been reawakened by global warming and toxic dumping, a nightmare the government tried to keep submerged. Neptune's Reckoning. Terror knows no depth

CHECK OUT OTHER GREAT DEEP SEA THRILLERS

SEA RAPTOR
by John J. Rust

From terrorist hunter to monster hunter! Jack Rastun was a decorated U.S. Army Ranger, until an unfortunate incident forced him out of the service. He is soon hired by the Foundation for Undocumented Biological Investigation and given a new mission, to search for cryptids, creatures whose existence has not been proven by mainstream science. Teaming up with the daring and beautiful wildlife photographer Karen Thatcher, they must stop a sea monster's deadly rampage along the Jersey Shore. But that's not the only danger Rastun faces. A group of murderous animal smugglers also want the creature. Rastun must utilize every skill learned from years of fighting, otherwise, his first mission for the FUBI might very well be his last.

OCEAN'S HAMMER
by D.J. Goodman

Something strange is happening in the Sea of Cortez. Whales are beaching for no apparent reason and the local hammerhead shark population, previously believed to be fished to extinction, has suddenly reappeared. Marine biologists Maria Quintero and Kevin Hoyt have come to investigate with a television producer in tow, hoping to get footage that will land them a reality TV show. The plan is to have a stand-off against a notorious illegal shark-fishing captain and then go home.

Things are not going according to plan.

There is something new in the waters of the Sea of Cortez. Something smart. Something huge. Something that has its own plans for Quintero and Hoyt.

Check out other great

Sea Monster Novels!

Edward J. McFadden III

SHADOW OF THE ABYSS

Out of the past comes an immense horror. An ancient creature that must feed its voracious hunger.A massive landslide on Grand Bahama Bank sends a thirty-foot wave traveling at 150MPH toward the east coast of Florida, and the tsunami drags in something horrible from the depths of the Mid-Atlantic Ridge rift valley. Now a monster roams Florida's east coast and its shallows, searching for prey.Matthew "Splinter" Woods lives in Sailfish Haven. He's a washed-out Navy SEAL who lives off the grid on his dilapidated boat and has withdrawn from society rather than face his demons. But when his ex-girlfriend, charter boat captain Lenah Brisbee, comes to him for help, Splinter gets drawn into a battle that pits him against the strongest enemy he's ever faced as he races against time to find the monster before it turns the vaters he loves blood red.

Michael Cole

MEGALODON VS COLOSSAL SNAKE

Brought to life by the miracle of DNA cloning, a 93-foot Megalodon shark has escaped captivity. With an insatiable appetite and unmatched aggression, it travels west for the Georgia coast, leaving a path of destruction in its wake. Bullets and harpoons can't penetrate it, steel nets can't hold it, and it's only a matter of time before the whole world finds out about it. In a race to stop the beast, the organization responsible recruit a marine biologist and a herpetologist to develop a plan to catch it. To do it, they must unleash the company's other genetically modified experiment—a 150-foot snake, resurrected from the DNA of the mighty Titanoboa. The pursuit leads to inevitable combat, and the scientists are forced to witness the deadly realities of genetic tampering. As the battle escalates, it is clear nobody is safe...and that nature never intended for these beasts to return. As the destruction mounts, and the death toll climbs, the true loser of Megalodon vs. Colossal Snake is humanity.

www.ingramcontent.com/pod-product-compliance
Lightning Source LLC
Chambersburg PA
CBHW072238190626
46809CB00018B/2848

* 9 7 8 1 9 2 3 6 6 3 0 1 5 *